Pigeon Pie

Also by Nancy Mitford

Novels
HIGHLAND FLING
CHRISTMAS PUDDING
WIGS ON THE GREEN
THE PURSUIT OF LOVE
LOVE IN A COLD CLIMATE
THE BLESSING
DON'T TELL ALFRED

Non-Fiction
MADAME DE POMPADOUR
VOLTAIRE IN LOVE
THE SUN KING
FREDERICK THE GREAT
THE WATER BEETLE (essays)

Edited
THE LADIES OF ALDERLEY
THE STANLEYS OF ALDERLEY
NOBLESSE OBLIGE

Pigeon Pie

BY

NANCY MITFORD

HAMISH HAMILTON
LONDON

First published in Great Britain 1940
by Hamish Hamilton Limited
90 Great Russell Street London WC1B 3PT
First published in this edition 1976

Printed and bound in Great Britain by
Redwood Burn Limited
Trowbridge & Esher

Chapter One

SOPHIA GARFIELD had a clear mental picture of what the outbreak of war was going to be like. There would be a loud bang, succeeded by inky darkness and a cold wind. Stumbling over heaps of rubble and dead bodies, Sophia would search with industry, but without hope, for her husband, her lover and her dog. It was in her mind like the End of the World, or the Last Days of Pompeii, and for more than two years now she had been steeling herself to bear with fortitude the hardships, both mental and physical, which must accompany this cataclysm.

However, nothing in life happens as we expect, and the outbreak of the great war against Hitlerism certainly did not happen according to anybody's schedule except possibly Hitler's own. In fact, Sophia was driving in her Rolls-Royce through one of those grey and nondescript towns on the border between England and Scotland when, looking out of the window, she saw a man selling newspapers; the poster which he wore as an apron had scrawled upon it in pencil the words WAR BEGUN. As this was on the 31st of August, 1939, the war which had begun was the invasion of Poland by Germany; the real war, indeed, did begin more pompously, if not more in accordance with preconceived ideas, some four days later. There was no loud bang, but Mr. Chamberlain said on the wireless what a bitter blow it had been for him, and then did his best to relieve the tension by letting off air-raid sirens. It sounded very nice and dramatic, though a few citizens, having supposed that their last hour was at hand, were slightly annoyed by this curious practical joke.

Sophia's war began in that border town. She felt rather shivery when she saw the poster, and said to Rawlings, her chauffeur, 'Did you see?' and Rawlings said, 'Yes, m'lady, I did.' Then they passed by a hideous late-Victorian church, and the whole population of the town seemed to be occupied in propping it up with sandbags. Sophia, who had never seen a sandbag before, began to cry, partly from terror and partly because it rather touched her to see anybody taking so much trouble over a church so ugly that it might have been specially made for bombs. Further along the road in a small, grey village, a band of children, with labels round their necks and bundles in their arms, were standing by a motor-bus. Most of them were howling. Rawlings volunteered the remark that he had never expected to see refugees in England, that Hitler was a red swine, and he would like to get his hands on him. At a garage where they stopped for petrol the man said that we could never have held up our heads if we hadn't finished it now.

When they got to Carlisle, Sophia decided that she must go on by train to London. She had been on the road already for ten hours, and was miserably stiff, but having arranged to help with the evacuation of mothers and children, she was due at a school in the Commercial Road at eight o'clock the following morning. Accordingly, she told Rawlings to stay the night at Carlisle, and she herself boarded the London train. There were no sleepers, the train was full of drunken soldiers, and it was blacked out. Some journeys remain in the memory as a greater nightmare even than bad illness; this was to be one of them. Sophia was lucky to secure a seat, as people were standing in the corridors; she did so, however, sharing the carriage with a Scotch officer, his very young wife, a nasty middle-aged lady and several sleeping men. The nasty lady and the officer's wife both had puppies with them, which surprised Sophia. She had wrenched herself away from her own Milly that morning, unwilling to have an extra object of search among the rubble and corpses. Soon total darkness descended, and fellow-passengers became mere shadowy forms and voices assuming ghost-like proportions.

The officer's wife went to the lavatory, and the little officer said confidentially to Sophia, 'We were only married on Saturday, and she's verra upset,' which made Sophia cry again. She supposed she was going to spend the war in rivers of tears, being an easy crier. The nasty lady now said that it seemed foolish to go to war for Poland, but nobody bothered to take up the point.

'You mark my words,' she said, 'this will mean a shilling on the income tax.'

Whether or not it be true that drowning persons are treated to a cinematograph show of their past lives, it is certainly a fact that during fiendish journeys undertaken with no cheerful object in view most people's

3

thoughts are inclined to take on that drowning aspect either with regard to past or future events. Sophia, achingly tired, but unable to go to sleep, began to re-enact in her mind scenes from her past life.

The only child of a widowed peer, who could write his name, Maida Vale, but little else, she had seen London for the first time at the age of eighteen. An aunt had then taken her out in the world. She fell under the influence of Maurice Baring's novels, her ideal hero was a suave, perhaps slightly bald, enormously cultivated diplomat. Gentlemen of this description did not abound at the balls she went to, and the callow youths of twenty who did, were a source of disillusionment to her. She was not shy and she had high spirits, but she was never a romper and therefore never attained much popularity with the very young. At the end of her first London season, she went to a large house-party for Goodwood, and here one of her fellow-guests was Luke Garfield. He had just left the diplomatic service to go into the City. His very pompous, cultivated manner, excellent clothes, knowledge of foreign affairs and slight baldness gave him prestige in the eyes of Sophia, and he became her hero. On the other hand, Luke saw at once that her charm and unusual looks would be invaluable to him in his career, and in so far as he was capable of such a warm-blooded emotion, he fell in love with the girl. He proposed to her the following November, after she had poured out tea for him in her aunt's drawing-room. His pin-stripe trousers and perfect restraint seemed to her quite ideal, the whole scene

4

could have come out of 'Cat's Cradles', and was crowned for her by Luke's suggestion that their honeymoon should be spent in Rome where he had recently been *en poste*.

How soon she began to realize that he was a pompous prig she could not remember. He was a sight-seeing bore, and took her the Roman rounds with a dutiful assiduity, and without ever allowing her to sit on a stone and use her eyes. Her jokes annoyed and never amused him; when she said that all the sights in Rome were called after London cinemas, he complained that she was insular, facetious and babyish. She was insular, really; she loved England and never thought abroad was worth the trouble it took getting there. Luke spoke Italian in such a dreadfully affected way that it embarrassed her to hear him.

It was on her honeymoon in Rome that she first met Rudolph Jocelyn. He made no great impression on her, being the antithesis of what she then so much admired. He was not bald, suave, or in any sense of the word a diplomat. On the contrary, he had a shock of tow-coloured hair, spoke indistinctly, dressed badly, and was always in a great hurry. Luke disapproved of him; he said that Jocelyn's journalistic activities were continually getting the Embassy in trouble with the Italians. Besides, he kept low company and looked disreputable, and the fact that he spoke Italian like a native, and two dialects as well, failed to endear him to Luke. Some months later Sophia heard that he had mobilized the Italian army in a moment of lightheartedness; his newspaper splashed the martial news,

5

and Rudolph Jocelyn was obliged to abandon journalism as a career.

Sophia had a happy character and was amused by life; if she was slightly disillusioned she was by no means unhappy in her marriage. Luke was as cold as a fish and a great bore; soon however she began to regard him as a great joke, and as she liked jokes she became quite fond of him when, which happened soon, she fell out of love with him. Also she saw very little of him. He left the house before she was properly awake in the morning, returning only in time to dress for dinner, then they dined out. Every Saturday to Monday they stayed with friends in the country. Sophia often spent weeks at a time with her father, in Worcestershire or Scotland. Luke seemed to be getting very rich. About twice a week he obliged her to entertain or be entertained by insufferably boring business people, generally Americans. He explained that this must be regarded as her work so she acquiesced meekly, but unfortunately she was not very good at her work, as Luke never hesitated to tell her. He said that she treated the wives of these millionaires as if they were cottage women and she a visiting duchess. He said they were unused to being treated with condescension by the wives of much poorer men, who hoped to do business with their husbands. Sophia could not understand all this; she thought she was being wonderful to them, but they seemed to her a strange species.

'I simply don't see the point of getting up at six all the time you are young and working eighteen hours a day in order to be a millionaire, and then when you are

6

a millionaire still getting up at six and working eighteen hours a day, like Mr. Holst. And poor Mrs. Holst, who has got up at six too all these years, so that now she can't sleep on in the morning, only has the mingiest little diamond clip you ever saw. What does it all mean?'

Luke said something about big business and not tying up your capital. Mr. Holst was the head of the firm of which Luke's was the London office, and the Holst visits to England were a nightmare for Sophia. She was obliged to see a great deal of Mrs. Holst on these occasions and to listen by the hour to her accounts of their early struggles as well as to immense lectures on business ethics.

'Lady Sophia,' Mrs. Holst would say, fingering her tiny diamond clip, 'I hope that you and Sir Luke fully realize that Mr. Holst has entrusted his good name—for the good of the business, Lady Sophia, is the good name of Mr. Holst, and in fact Mr. Holst has often said to me that Mr. Holst's business is Mr. Holst—well, as I was saying, this good name is entrusted into Sir Luke's keeping and into your keeping, Lady Sophia. I always say a business man's wife should be Caesar's wife. As I have told you, Lady Sophia, Mr. Holst worked for twenty hours a day for thirty years to build up this business. Often and often I have heard him say "My home is my office and my office is my home" and that, Lady Sophia, is the profound truth. Now, as I was saying . . .' and so it went on.

Sophia, who was never able to get it out of her head that the City was a large room in which a lot of men sat all day doing sums, and who was of course quite unable to distinguish between stock-brokers, bill-brokers, bankers and jobbers, found these lectures almost as incomprehensible as the fact that Mrs. Holst should take so much interest in her husband's profession when it had only produced, for her, such a wretched little diamond clip. Sophia loved jewels, she had fortunately inherited very beautiful ones of her own from her mother, and Luke, who was not at all mean, often added to them when he had brought off a deal.

The train stopped. The Scotch officer, his wife, the nasty lady and their puppies all got out. It was one o'clock in the morning. The carriage then filled up, from the corridor which was packed, with very young private soldiers. They were very drunk, singing over and over again a dirty little song about which bits of Adolph they were going to bring back with them. They all ended by passing out, two with their heads in Sophia's lap. She was too tired to remove them, and so they lay snoring hot breath on to her for the rest of the journey.

Her thoughts continued. After some years of marriage Luke had joined the Boston Brotherhood, one of those new religions which are wafted to us every six months or so across the Atlantic. At first she had suspected that he found it very profitable in the way of deals with other Brothers; presently however he became earnest. He inaugurated week-end parties in their London house, which meant a hundred people to every meal, great jolly queues waiting outside the lavatories, public confessions in the drawing-room, and quiet times in the housemaid's cupboard. Sophia had not been very lady-like about all this, and in fact had played a double game in order to get the full benefit of it. She allowed people to come clean all over her, and even came clean herself in a perfectly shameless way, combing the pages of Freud for new sins with which to fascinate the Brotherhood. So, of course, they loved her. It was just at this time that everything in Sophia's life began to seem far more amusing because of Rudolph Jocelyn whom she had fallen in love with. He came to all the week-end parties, tea parties, fork luncheons and other celebrations of the newest Christianity, and Luke dis-liked him as much as ever but endured him in a cheery Brotherly way, regarding him no doubt as a kind of penance, sent to chasten, as well as a brand to be snatched from the burning. Brothers, like Roman Catholics, get a bonus for souls.

Sophia and Rudolph loved each other very much. This does not mean that it had ever occurred to them to alter the present situation, which seemed exactly to suit all parties; Rudolph was unable to visualize him-self as a married man, and Sophia feared that divorce, re-marriage and subsequent poverty would not bring out the best in her character. As for Luke, he took up with a Boston Brotherly soulmate called Florence, and was perfectly contented with matters as they stood. Florence, he realized, would not show to the same advantage as Sophia when he was entertaining prospec-tive clients; Sophia might not be ideally tactful with their wives, but she did radiate an atmosphere of security and of the inevitability of upper-class status

9

quo. Florence, however saintly, did not. Besides that, Luke was hardly the kind of man to favour divorce. Middle-aged, rather fat and very rich, he would look ridiculous, he knew, if his wife ran away with a poor, handsome and shabby young man. Let it be whispered too that Luke and Sophia, after so many years, were really rather attached to each other.

As she sat in the train reviewing her past life, Sophia felt absolutely certain that it was now over and done with. It lay behind her, while she, with every revolution of the wheels, was being carried towards that loud bang, those ruins, corpses and absence of loved ones. She had been taken very much unawares by the war, staying with her father in a remote part of Scotland where telephone and radio were unknown, and where the newspapers were often three days late. Now in the blacked-out train crowded with soldiers, she was already enveloped by it. The skies of London were probably dark by now with enemy planes, but apprehension was of so little use that she concentrated upon the happiness of her past life. The future must look after her in its own way. She became drowsy, and her mind filled with images. The first meet she ever went to, early in the morning with her father's agent. She often remembered this, and it had become a composite picture of all the cub-hunting she had ever done, the autumn woods and the smell of bonfires, dead leaves and hot horses. Riding home from the last meet of a season, late in the afternoon of a spring day, there would be prim-roses and violets under the hedges, far far away the sound of a horn, and later an owl. The world is not a bad place, it is a pity to have to die. But, of course, it is only a good place for a very few people. Think of Dachau, think of China, and Czechoslovakia and Spain. Think of the distressed areas. We must die now, and there must be a new world. Sophia went to sleep and only woke up at Euston. She went to the station hotel, had a bath, and arrived at the Commercial Road at exactly eight o'clock. Of the day which followed she had afterwards but little recollection. The women from London were wonderful, their hostesses in the country extremely disagreeable. It was a sad business.

When it was over Sophia went to bed and slept for thirteen hours.

Chapter Two

SHE got up in time for luncheon. There had been no loud bang, the house was not in ruins, and when she rang her bell Greta, her German maid, appeared.

'Oh Greta, I thought you would have gone.'

'Gone, Frau Gräfin?'

Arguments and persuasion from Sophia failed to prevent Greta from calling her this.

'Back to Germany.'

'Oh no, Frau Gräfin; Sir Luke says there will be no war. Our good Führer will not make war on England.'

Sophia was rather bored. She had never liked Greta and had not expected to find her still there. She asked whether Sir Luke was in, and was told yes, and that he had ordered luncheon for four. It was a very hot day, and she put on a silk dress which, owing to the cold summer, she had hitherto been unable to wear.

Rudolph was in the drawing-room making a cocktail.

'I say, have you seen Florence? God has guided her to dye her hair.'

'No—what colour—where is she?'

'Orange. Downstairs,' he said, pulling Sophia towards him with the hand which did not hold the cocktail shaker, and kissing her. 'How are you?'

'Very pleased to see you, my darling. It seemed a long time.'

Florence appeared, followed by Luke. Her hair,

which had been brown, was indeed a rich marmalade, and she was rather smartly dressed in printed crepe-de-chine, though the dress did not look much when seen near Sophia's.

'Have a drink,' said Rudolph, pouring them out. Florence gave him a tortured, jolly smile, and said that drinking gave her extraordinarily little pleasure nowadays. Luke, who hated being offered drinks in his own house, refused more shortly. 'Lunch is ready,' he said.

They went downstairs.

'Has the war begun?' asked Sophia, wondering who could have ordered soup for luncheon, and seeing in this the God-guided hand of Florence. She guessed that Florence was staying in the house.

'No,' said Rudolph. 'I don't know what we're waiting for.'

'My information is,' said Luke, at which Rudolph gave a great wink, because Luke so often used those words and his information was so often not quite correct, 'my information is that Our Premier (his voice here took on a reverent note) is going to be able to save the peace again. At a cost, naturally. We shall have to sacrifice Poland, of course, but I hear that the Poles are in a very bad way, rotten with Communism, you know, and they will be lucky to have Herr Hitler to put things right there. Then we may have to give him some colony or other, and of course a big loan.'

'What about the Russian pact?' said Rudolph.

'Means nothing—absolutely nothing. Herr Hitler will never allow the Bolsheviks into Europe. No, I don't feel any alarm. We have no quarrel with Germany that

Our Premier and Herr Hitler together cannot settle peacefully.'

Sophia said shortly, 'Well, if they do, and there isn't a revolution here as the result, I shall leave this country for ever and live somewhere else, that's all. But I won't believe it.'

Then, remembering from past experience that such conversations were not only useless but also led to ill-feeling, she changed the subject. She had never been so near parting from Luke as at the time of Munich, when, in his eyes, Our Premier had moved upon the same exalted sphere as Brother Bones, founder of the Boston Brotherhood, and almost you might say, God. His information then had been that the Czechs were in a very bad way, rotten with Communism, and would be lucky to have Herr Hitler to put things right. It also led him to believe that universal disarmament would follow the Munich agreement, and that the Sudetenland was positively Hitler's last territorial demand in Europe. Carlyle has said that identity of sentiment but difference of opinion are the known elements of pleasant dialogue. The dialogue in many English homes at that time was very far from pleasant.

'Then a silly old welfare-worker came up to a woman with eight coal-black children and said, "You haven't got a yellow label, so you can't be pregnant," and the woman said, "Can't I? Won't the dad be pleased to hear that now?" And when we got to the village green the parson was waiting to meet us, and he looked at the pregnant ladies and said, very sadly, "To think that *one man* is responsible for all this." It's absolutely true.'

Rudolph watched her with admiration. He enjoyed Sophia's talent for embroidering on her own experiences, and the way she rushed from hyperbole to hyperbole, ending upon a wild climax of improbability with the words 'It's absolutely true.' According to Sophia, she could hardly move outside her house without encountering the sort of adventure that only befalls the ordinary person once in a lifetime. Her narrative always had a basis of truth, and this was an added fascination for Rudolph who amused himself by trying to separate fact from fiction.

'Darling Sophia,' he said, as she came to the end of a real tour de force about her father, whom she had left, she said, blackening the pebbles of his drive which he considered would be particularly visible from the air, 'I know what your job will be in the war—taking German spies out to luncheon and telling them what you believe to be the truth. When you look them in the eye and say "I promise it's absolutely true", they'll think it's gospel because it'll be so obvious that you do yourself. The authorities will simply tell you the real truth, and you'll do the rest for them.'

'Oh, Rudolph, what a glamorous idea!'

She took Florence upstairs. Florence wriggled a good deal which she always did if she felt embarrassed, and in spite of her conscious superiority in the moral sphere she often felt embarrassed with Sophia. Presently she said in a loud, frank voice, 'I hope it's all right, Sophia. I'm staying here.'

'Oh, good. I hope you're comfortable. If you want any ironing done, just tell Greta.'

15

Florence said she required extraordinarily little maiding, but this did not for a moment deceive Sophia, who had been told by Greta, in a burst of confidence, that Fraulein Turnbull gave more trouble than three of the Frau Gräfin.

Florence now drew a deep breath, always with her the prelude to an outburst of Christianity, and said that the times were very grave and that it made her feel sad to see people pay so little attention to their souls as Sophia and Rudolph.

'We don't think our rotten little souls so important as all that.'

'Ah but you see it isn't only your souls. Each person has a quantity of other souls converging upon his—that's what makes this life such a frightfully jolly adventure. In your case, Sophia, with your looks and position, you could influence directly and indirectly hundreds—yes, hundreds of people. Think how exciting that would be.'

Sophia saw that she was in for a sermon, and resigned herself. She knew from sad experience that to answer back merely encouraged the Brotherhood to fresh efforts.

'You know, dear, Luke feels it very much. It hurts him when you talk as you did at lunch, flippantly and with exaggeration. I wish you could realize how much happier it makes one to be perfectly truthful, even in little ways. Truth is a thing that adds so greatly to the value of human relationships.'

'Some,' said Sophia carelessly. 'Now it adds to the value of my relationship with Rudolph to tell more and funnier lies. He likes it.'

'I wonder if that sort of relationship is of much value. Personally the only people I care to be very intimate with are the ones you feel would make a good third if God asked you out to dinner.'

Sophia wished that Florence would not talk about the Almighty as if his real name was Godfrey, and God was just Florence's nickname for him.

'Oh, God would get on with Rudolph,' she said.

Florence smiled her bright, crucified smile, and said that she was sure there was good material in Rudolph if one knew where to look for it. Then she wriggled about and said, very loudly, 'Oh, Sophia, how much happier it would be for you, and for those about you, if you would give your sins to God. I feel there would be, oh! such a gay atmosphere in this house if you could learn to do just that.'

'Only one sin, Florence, such a harmless one. I don't steal, I honour my father, I don't covet, and 1 don't commit murder.'

'Perhaps flippancy is the worst sin of all.'

'I'm not flippant but I'm not religious and I never will be, not if I live to a hundred. It's a matter of temperament, you know.'

This was a false step. Florence now embarked on a rigmarole of bogus philosophy which no power short of an explosion could have stopped. Poor Sophia lay back and let it flow, which it did until the men came into the drawing-room, when Florence gave Luke a flash of her white and even teeth which all too clearly said 'I have failed again.'

'I'm just going up for a little quiet time,' she said.

'I'll be ready in half an hour.' She and Luke played golf on Saturday afternoons.

'I'm just going down for a little quiet time and I'll be ready in about half an hour,' said Rudolph, picking up the *Tatler*. When he got back, he said, 'Come along, Sophia, I'm taking you to the local A.R.P. office to get a job.'

'There won't be any war,' said Luke comfortably, as he settled down to his *Times*.

Sophia and Rudolph strolled out into the sunshine.

'Let's go to Kew,' said Sophia.

'Yes, we will when you have got your job.'

'Oh darling, oh dear, do I have to have a job?'

'Yes, you do, or I shall be through with you. You know that I think it's perfectly shameful the way you haven't done any training the last few months. Now you must get on with it quickly. There is only one justification for people like you in a community, and that is that they should pull their weight in a war. The men must fight and the women must be nurses.'

'Darling, I couldn't be a nurse. Florence has a first aid book and I looked inside and saw a picture of a knee. I nearly fainted. I can't bear knees, I've got a thing about them. I don't like ill people, either, and then I'm not so very strong, I should cockle. Tell you what— could I be a précis writer at the Foreign Office?'

'There haven't been précis writers at the Foreign Office since Lord Palmerston. Anyway, you couldn't work in a Government Department, you're far too mooney. If you can't bear knees and don't like ill people, you can scrub floors and wash up for those that can and do. Now here we are, go along and fix yourself up.'

Sophia found herself in a large empty house, empty, that is, of furniture, but full of would-be workers. She had to wait in a queue before being interviewed by a lady at a desk. The young man in front of her announced that he was a Czech, and not afraid of bombs. The lady said nor are British women afraid of bombs, which Sophia thought was going too far. She gave the young man an address to go to, and turned briskly to Sophia.

'Yes?' she said.

Sophia felt the shades of the prison-house closing in on her. She explained that she would do full-time voluntary work, but that she had no qualifications. For one wild moment of optimism she thought that the lady was going to turn her down. After looking through some papers, she said, however, 'Could you do office work in a First Aid Post?'

'I could try,' said Sophia doubtfully.

'Then take this note to Sister Wordsworth at St. Anne's Hospital First Aid Post. Thank you. Good day.'

Rudolph was in earnest conversation with a German Jew when she came out. On hearing that she was fixed up, he said that she might have a holiday before beginning her job. 'You can go to St. Anne's to-morrow,' he said. 'I'm taking you down to Kew now.'

They sat on a bench at the end of the ilex avenue and stared at Sion House across the river. Sophia asked

Rudolph what he planned to do, now that the war had begun.

'I hope for a commission, of course,' he said; 'failing that I shall enlist.'

'Somebody who knows all those languages could get a job at home—I mean not a fighting job. Perhaps it is your duty to do that,' she said hopefully.

'Can't help my duty; I'm going to fight Germans in this war—not Nazis, mind you, Germans. I mean huns.'

Sophia agreed with him really. The huns must be fought.

'How strange everything seems now that the war is here,' she said. 'I suppose it is unreal because we have been expecting it for so long now, and have known that it must be got over before we can go on with our lives. Like in the night when you want to go to the loo and it is miles away down a freezing cold passage and yet you know you have to go down that passage before you can be happy and sleep again. We are starting down it now. Oh, darling, I wish it was over and we were back in bed. What shall I do when you've gone?'

'Don't you anticipate,' said Rudolph severely; 'you never have, so don't begin now. You are the only person I know who lives entirely in the present, it is one of the attractive things about you.'

'If you are killed,' said Sophia, paying no attention.

'You are one of those lucky women with two strings to their bow. If I am killed, there is always old Luke.'

'Yes, but the point is I shall have such an awful grudge against Luke, don't you see? I do so fearfully think the war is the result of people like him, always rushing off abroad and pretending to those wretched foreigners that England will stand for anything. Cracking them up over here, too; Herr Hitler this, and Herr von Ribbentrop that, and bulwarks against Bolshevism and so on. Of course, the old fellow thought he was making good feeling, and probably he never even realized that the chief reason he loved the Germans was because they buttered him up so much. All those free rides in motors and aeroplanes.'

'You can't blame him,' said Rudolph, 'he never cut any ice over here, but as soon as he set foot in Germany he was treated as a minor royalty or something. Of course it was lovely for him. Why, Berlin has been full of people like that for years. The Germans were told to make a fuss of English people, so of course masses of English stampeded over there to be made a fuss of. But it never occurred to them that they were doing definite harm to their own country; they just got a kick out of saying "mein Führer" and being taken round in Mercedes-Benzes. All the same they weren't directly responsible for the war. Old Luke is all right, he's a decent old fellow at heart. I feel quite happy leaving you in his hands. I believe he's getting over the Brotherhood, too, you'll see.'

As they strolled across Kew Green to get a taxi, an unearthly yelp announced to them that they had been observed by Sophia's godfather, Sir Ivor King, and sure enough, there he was, the old fellow, waving a curly, butter-coloured wig at them out of his bedroom window. He invited them to come in for a cup of tea.

This faintly farcical old figure was the idol of the

British race, and reigned supreme in the hearts of his fellow-countrymen, indeed of music lovers all over the world, as the King of Song. In his heyday, he had been most famous as a singer of those sexy ballads which were adored by our grandparents, and for which most of us have a secret partiality. He was unrivalled, too, in opera. The unique quality of his voice was the fact that it could reach higher and also lower notes than have ever been reached before by any human being, some of which were so high that only bats, others so low that only horses, could hear them. When he was a very young man studying in Germany, his music teacher said to him, 'Herr King, you shall make, with that voice of yours, musical history. I hope I may live to hear you at your zenith.'

The prophecy came true. Ivor King was knighted at an early age, he made a large fortune, gained an unassailable position and the nickname by which he was always known, 'The King of Song', largely on the strength of this enormous range of voice. Largely, but not solely. A lovable and very strong personality, a genial quality of good fellowship, and latterly his enormous age, had played their part, and combined with his magnificent notes to make him not only one of the best known but also one of the best loved men of several successive generations. Among particular achievements he was the only man ever to sing the name part in the opera *Norma*, the script of which had been re-written especially for him, and re-named *Norman*.

The King of Song had toured the world, and particularly the Empire, dozens of times and these tours were indeed like royal progresses. In very remote parts of Africa the natives often mistook him for Queen Victoria's husband, and it was universally admitted that he had done more towards welding the Empire in the cultural sphere than any other individual. Quite bald, although with a marvellous selection of wigs, and finally quite toothless, he still maintained a gallant fight against old age, although some two years previously he had succumbed to the extent of giving a final farewell concert at the Albert Hall. He had then retired to a charming house on Kew Green, which he named Vocal Lodge, and devoted himself to botany; in the pursuit of this science, however, he was more keen than lucky.

'She wore a wreath of roses the day that first we met,' he chanted, cutting a seed cake. It was what the most vulgar of the many generations which had passed over his head would call his signature tune, and he sang it in a piercing soprano.

Sophia poured out tea, and asked after his Lesbian irises.

'They were not what they seemed,' he said, 'wretched things. I brought the roots all the way from Lesbos, as you know, and when they came up, what were they? Mere pansies. Too mortifying. And now I'm the air-raid warden for Kew Gardens, in a tin hat—and it will be years before I visit Greece again. It may be for years, and it may-hay be for ever. As you will note, the war has found me in excellent voice. I am singing at the Chiswick Town Hall to-night to our local decontamination squads. Such dear boys and girls. And let me darkly hint at a more exalted engagement in the not-too-too-

23

far-off future. I was trying to decide, when I saw you on the Green, whether I should go to my interview with some Important Personages as a blond or a brunette. I think I favour the butter-coloured curls,' he said, taking off his wig and revealing beneath a head of egg-like baldness.

Sophia and Rudolph were quite used to this, for the King's wigs were as much off as on, and there was never any kind of pretence about them being his own luxuriant hair.

'Yes, I have always liked that one,' said Sophia, 'it softens your features. What important personages?'

'Ah,' said the old singer, 'I can keep a secret. What are you up to, Rudolph? I haven't seen you since the Munich crisis. I may tell you that, having heard that you were doing the Italian broadcast from the B.B.C., I switched on the wireless to listen. Well, I said to Magdalen Beech, poor Rudolph sounds very ill—then we discovered that it was the dear late Pope, and not Rudolph at all.'

Sir Ivor was a fervent Roman Catholic. For a short time, many years ago, he had been married to a woman so pious and so lavish with Sir Ivor's money that she had posthumously been made a Papal Duchess and was accorded the unique honour of being buried in the Vatican gardens. Lady Beech was her sister.

'Now you can tell me something,' said Sophia, glancing at the Sargent portrait, in brown velvet and lace, of Duchess King which hung over the chimneypiece. 'I had a letter from Lady Beech saying what a pity, as we must all so soon be dead, that we shouldn't all be

24

going on to the same place afterwards. What really happens to us heretics, darling old gentleman?'

'Darling pretty young lady, you pop straight on to a gridiron and there you baste to eternity.'

'Baste?' said Sophia.

'Baste. Whenever I have time, perhaps say once in a million years, I will bring you a drop of water on the end of my finger. Apart from this, your pleasures will be few and simple.'

'What I'm wondering is,' said Rudolph, 'how much you and Lady Beech will enjoy such purely Catholic society for so uninterrupted a spell?'

At dinner that night, Luke's information was that a huge scheme of appeasement, world-wide in its implications, was even now being worked out. He said the wretched Socialists were not making things easy for Our Premier, but that he was too big a man and the scheme too big a scheme to be thwarted by pinpricks in Parliament. Parliament and the Press might have to be got rid of for a time whilst Our Premier and Herr Hitler rearranged the world. In any case, there would be no war. The next morning poor Luke was so wretched that Sophia felt quite sorry for him. He really seemed astounded that Herr Hitler should be prepared to risk all those wonderful swimming-pools in a major war.

When the Prime Minister's Speech and hoax air-raid warning were over, Sophia went round to report at the First Aid Post. Here, in a large garage under St. Anne's Hospital, cold, damp and dirty, pretty Sister Wordsworth was bringing order out of confusion. She really

25

seemed pleased to engage Sophia, in spite of her lack of qualifications, and told her that she could come every day from one to seven. The work was simple. Sophia was to sit behind a partition of sacking, labelled Office, to answer the telephone, count the washing and do various odd jobs. In the case of raids, Sister Wordsworth assured her that while she might have to see knee joints, she would have no intimate contact with them.

Henceforward Sophia's life was sharply divided in two parts, her life behind the gasproof flap of the First Aid Post and her own usual unhampered life outside. Sometimes she rather enjoyed her sacking life, sometimes she felt that she could hardly endure it. The cold stuffy atmosphere got on her nerves, she was unaccustomed to sitting still for hours on end, and what work there was to do, such as counting washing, she did not do very well. On the other hand, she liked all the people in the Post, and habit once having gripped her, as it does so soon in life, she became quite resigned and regarded the whole thing completely as a matter of course.

Chapter Three

RATHER soon after the war had been declared, it became obvious that nobody intended it to begin. The belligerent countries were behaving like children in a round game, picking up sides, and until the sides had been picked up the game could not start.

England picked up France, Germany picked up Italy. England beckoned to Poland, Germany answered with Russia. Then Italy's Nanny said she had fallen down and grazed her knee, running, and mustn't play. England picked up Turkey, Germany picked up Spain, but Spain's Nanny said she had internal troubles, and must sit this one out. England looked towards the Oslo group, but they had never played before, except little Belgium, who had hated it, and the others felt shy. America, of course, was too much of a baby for such a grown-up game, but she was just longing to see it played. And still it would not begin.

The party looked like being a flop, and everybody was becoming very much bored, especially the Americans who are so fond of blood and entrails. They were longing for the show, and with savage taunts, like boys at a bull-baiting from behind safe bars, they urged that it should begin at once. The pit-side seats for which they had paid so heavily in printer's ink were turning out to be a grave disappointment; they sat in them, chewing gum, stamping their feet and shouting in unison, 'This war is phoney.'

Week after week went by. People made jokes about how there was the Boer War, and then the Great War, and then the Great Bore War. They said Hitler's secret weapon was boredom. Sophia hoped it was. She had long cherished a conviction that Hitler's secret weapon was an aerial torpedo addressed to Lady Sophia Garfield, 98 Granby Gate, S.W., and she very much preferred boredom.

Sophia had two friends in the Cabinet. They were called Fred and Ned, and as a matter of fact while Fred was in the Cabinet, Ned had not yet quite reached that sixth form of politicians and was only in the Government, but Sophia could not distinguish between little details like that, and to her they were 'My friends in the Cabinet'. She often dined with the two of them and found these evenings very enjoyable because, although they both had young and pretty wives, it seems that the wives of Cabinet Ministers race, so to speak, under different rules from ordinary women, and never expect to see their husbands except in bed if they share one. So Sophia had Fred and Ned to herself on these occasions. As she liked both male and female company, but did not much like it mixed, this arrangement suited her nicely.

They took her to dine at the Carlton, and talked a great deal about the political prospects of their various acquaintances, and it was talk which Sophia was very much accustomed to, because it had begun years ago, when she was a young married woman taking Fred and Ned out to tea at the Cockpit; only then it had been a question of Pop and coloured waistcoats, and the Headmaster in those days had delivered his harangues in Chapel instead of on the floor of the House. She told them all about her Post, and Ned wrote things down in a notebook, and promised that A.R.P. should be reconstructed on the exact lines suggested by Sophia. She knew from experience how much that meant. Then Fred asked her if Luke was in the Tower yet, and this annoyed her because, while it was one thing to say to Rudolph in the privacy of Kew Gardens that Luke was an awful old fascist, it was quite another to have Fred, that ardent upholder of Munich, being facetious about him; so she turned on poor Fred with great vigour, and gave him a brisk résumé of the achievements of the National Government. She very nearly made him cry, and was just coming nicely into her stride over the National Liberals, of whom Fred was one, when Ned came loyally to his rescue saying 'Ah, but you haven't heard of Fred's wonderful scheme, all his own idea, for fixing Dr. Goebbels.' And he proceeded to outline the scheme.

It appeared that Fred's idea, his own unaided brainwave, was to invite Sir Ivor King, the King of Song, to conduct a world-wide campaign of songful propaganda.

'Harness his personality, as it were,' Fred explained, warming to his subject, 'to our cause. He's the only chap who could bring it off, and it would be wicked not to use him—why, he is one of our great natural advantages, you might say, like—well coal, or being an island. They've got nobody to touch him over there. Now my idea is that he should give out a special news bulletin every day, strongly flavoured with propaganda, of course, followed by a programme of song. See the point? People will switch on to hear him sing (the first time for two years, you know), and then they won't be able to help getting an earful of propaganda. We'll have him singing with the troops, singing with the air force, singing with the navy, jolly, popular stuff which the listeners all over the world can join in. You know how people like roaring out songs when they know the words. Besides, the man in the street has a great respect for old Ivor, great.'

According to Fred, he and the man in the street were as one, which was strange, considering that, except for the High Street, Windsor and The Turl, he had hardly ever been in a street.

'When you say listeners all over the world can join in, you mean English listeners?' said Sophia. She wanted to get the thing straight.

'By no means,' said Fred, eagerly, 'because, you see, the strength of this scheme is that it will be world-wide. I confess that, to begin with, I forgot that it's not everybody who can speak English. Then of course I remembered that there are Chinks and Japs and Fuzzy Wuzzies and Ice Creamers and Dagos, and so on. Ah! but we can overcome that difficulty. Is there any reason why he shouldn't learn to make those extraordinary sounds which they think of as music? Of course not. No. The old chappie is full of brains and enterprise—take on anything we ask him to, you bet.' And Fred began to give what he thought an excellent imitation of un-English music, nasal sounds of a painful quality. A county family who were dining at the next table told each other that this could not be the Minister for Propaganda, after all. Ned beat two forks together as an accompaniment, and they assured each other that neither was that the Member (so promising, such a career before him) for East Wessex.

'The old King is coming to my office to-morrow. I am seeing him myself,' Fred continued, when this horrid cacophony came to an end.

'He will be wearing his curly, butter-coloured wig,' said Sophia.

'We must see that he has a black one made. Don't want any Aryan nonsense in my scheme—I always think Propaganda is awfully un-English, anyway, but what I say, if you have it at all, for the Lord's sake have it good. And, by the way, Sophie, this is all most fearfully hush-hush, you know. Leakage and all that—not a word to Luke or anybody. The element of surprise is vital to the scheme.'

'I see, the old gentleman is your answer to Hitler's secret weapon.'

'I wouldn't go quite so far as that, but I can tell you we are expecting some pretty fruity results. I mean it's a world-wide scheme you see, not just a pettifogging little affair confined to England. And by the way,' he got out a notebook, 'I must remember to tell the police they had better keep an eye on the chap. Think what a coup for the Huns if he got bumped off or anything; I should never get over it.'

Sophia rang up her enemy. Olga Gogothsky (née Baby Bagg) had been her enemy since they were both aged ten. It was an intimate enmity which gave Sophia more pleasure than most friendships; she made sacrifices upon its altar and fanned the flames with assiduity.

'Hullo, my darling Sophie,' Olga purred, in the foreign accent which she had cultivated since just before her marriage and which was in striking contrast with the Eton and Oxford tones (often blurred by drink but always unmistakable) of Prince Gogothsky. 'Yes, I have been back a fortnight; such a journey, darling. And where did you go for the summer? Just quietly with dear Lord Maida Vale? Delicious. Me? Oh, poor little me, I had a very banal time with Pauline Mallory you know, the poetess, in her villa at Antibes. Crowds and crowds of people, parties, nothing else. You can imagine how that palled on me, dearest. Happily my beloved old Ambassador was there. He has her little villa, in the garden, and there he writes his memories. He is sweet enough to say that I inspire him in his work; he read it to me—so interesting, and written, how can I express it, with such art. The old days at the Montenegrin Court—so picturesque. You can imagine. Then Baroness von Bülop was a great friend of his, and he told me some fascinating things about her and her beautiful aunt which were rather too *intime* for cold, cold print. Well, what else—oh yes, Torchon was painting my portrait—he sees me as a Turkish slave girl which is very interesting because when Fromenti cast my horoscope he said that is what I used to be in one of my former lives. (In the Sultan's harem, I was his favourite wife.) Besides all this, I managed to get in a little writing, so you see my time was not quite wasted after all.'

Olga's writing was an interesting phenomenon, rather like the Emperor's new clothes. She let it be known that she was a poetess, and whenever, which was often, her photograph appeared in the illustrated press, the caption underneath would announce that very soon a slender volume might be expected from her pen. Sometimes even the subject-matter would be touched upon: 'Princess Serge Gogothsky, who is at present engaged upon a series of bird studies in verse.'

'This beautiful visitor to our shores is a lady of great talent. The long epic poem on Savonarola from her pen will soon be ready for publication,' and so on.

Once, for several weeks on end, Olga sat alone every evening at a special table at the Café Royal and wrote feverishly upon sheets of foolscap which she tore up, with an expression of agony on her face, just before closing time. Her work always seemed to be in progress rather than in print.

Sophia asked what she was doing as war work.

'Dearest, I must tell you that it's a secret. However, when you hear that I have an appointment under the Government, that I have to undertake great responsibilities, and that I may often be called out in the middle of the night without any idea of where I am to go, you may guess the kind of thing it is. More I cannot say.'

'Sounds to me like a certified midwife,' said Sophia crossly. It was really too much if old Baby Bagg was going to assume the rôle of beautiful female spy, while she herself had drearily admitted to working in a First Aid Post, all boredom and no glamour. Olga lied with such accomplishment that there were some people who believed in her tarradiddles, and Sophia had often been told what a talent for verse, what a delightful touch the Princess had.

'No, darling—what a charming joke, by the way, I must remember to tell my dear Chief. No, not a midwife. Though I'm sure it must be far far more exhausting, my Chief is a regular slave driver.'

'Oh, you have a Chief?'

'I only wish I could tell you Who it is. But there must be no leakage. What a wonderful man to work with— what magnetism, what finesse and what a brain! I must allow I am fortunate to be with him, and then the work is fascinating, vital. What if it does half kill me? There, I mustn't talk about myself. Tell me, what are you doing in this cruel war?'

Sophia said that she too had an important job under the Government.

'Really, my darling, have you? A First Aid Post, or something like that, I suppose?'

'Ah well, that's only what I tell people, actually of course it is an excellent blind for my real work. I wonder you don't adopt this idea, say you are working in a canteen, for instance. I'll forget what you've just told me if you like, and spread it round about the canteen!'

'Delicate little me!' cried Olga, 'in a canteen! But darling, who would ever believe such an unlikely thing —they would at once suspect goodness knows what. Well, dearest, I see the Chief waiting for me in his great car with the flag and priority notices, I shall feel quite important as we whirl away to Whitehall. I must fly, darling. Good-bye. I will visit you very soon in your little First Aid Post. Good-bye.'

Sophia then telephoned to her friend, Mary Pencill.

'Now, Mary, listen. You've got to come and work in my First Aid Post,' she said. 'It's perfect heaven. You can't think what heaven Sister Wordsworth is.'

'No, thank you, Sophie. I don't intend to work for this war in any way. I don't approve of it, you see.' Mary belonged to the extreme Left.

'Gracious, just like Luke. He doesn't approve of it either, nor does Florence. You are in awful company. So why are you in this awful company?'

'I can't help it if Luke happens to be right for once. It's sure to be for the wrong reasons if he is. All I know is that everything decent and worth supporting has been thrown away—Spain, Czechoslovakia, and now we're supposed to be fighting for the Poles, frightful people who knout their peasants. Actually, of course, it's simply the British Empire and our own skins as usual.'

'I'm fond of my skin,' said Sophia, 'and personally I think the British Empire is worth fighting for.'

'You can't expect me to think so. Why, look at our Government. Your friends Fred and Ned, for instance, are just as bad as Hitler, exactly the same thing. What is the use of fighting Hitler when there are people like

35

Ned and Fred here? We should do some cleaning up at home first.'

'Anyway, it's Hitler and Stalin now, don't forget the wedding bells.'

Mary had gone P.O.U.M., so she grudgingly conceded this point. 'Ned and Fred are practically the same people as Hitler and Stalin,' she said.

'I never heard anything so silly. Poor Fred and Ned. Well, I mean the proof of the pudding is in the eating. Just suppose now that the Ministry of Information had forgotten to tell us we had been beaten, and one day in Harrods we saw a little crowd gathering, and when we went to look it was Hitler and Stalin. Think how we should scream.'

'I expect you would.'

'So would you. Now, my point is, I often see Fred and Ned in Harrods, and I don't scream at all, I just say "Hullo duckie" or something. See the difference?'

'No, Sophia,' said Mary disapprovingly, 'I'm afraid you don't understand the principle.' She loved Sophia but thought her incurably frivolous.

'Another thing,' she said; 'why have you left the Left Book Club?'

'Darling, I only joined to please you.'

'That's no answer.'

'Well, if you want to know it's because the books are left.'

'Sophia!'

'I don't mean because they are Left and I can't get Evelyn Waugh or any of the things I want to read. I mean because they are left lying about the house.

Ordinary libraries like Harrods take them away when one has finished with them. I don't want the place cluttered up with books, so I have left. See?'

'Really, your life is bounded by Harrods.'

'Yes, it is rather. I had rather a horrid dream, though, about its being full of parachutists; my life is slightly bounded by them now, to tell you the truth, I think they are terrifying.'

'Nonsense, they would be interned.'

'That's what Luke says. Still the idea of those faces floating past one's bedroom window is rather unpleasant, you must admit.'

'By the way, I saw Rudolph last night coming out of the Empire with that foreign woman.'

'Who?'

'The one who always wears star-spangled yashmaks.'

'Oh, you mean Olga Gogothsky; she's no more foreign than you or me—although she does pretend to have Spanish blood, I believe.'

'Really—Government or Franco?'

'Baby Bagg. You must remember her at dances.' Sophia was only fairly pleased to hear that Olga had been out with Rudolph, who had announced that he was going to play bridge at his club.

'Anyhow, she looks too stupid.'

'She has just told me that she has got an important job under the Government, I simply must find out what it is.'

'First Aid Post, probably,' said Mary. 'You haven't told me yet what you do in yours?'

'Well, it sounds rather lugubrious but I absolutely

love it. I have an indelible pencil, you see, and when people are brought in dying and so on, I write on their foreheads.'

'Good gracious me, what do you write?'

'M for male and F for female, according to which they are, and a number. That's for the Ministry of Pensions. Then, for the doctor, how many doses of morphia and castor oil and so on they have had.'

'What an awful idea. What happens if you get a negro—or a neanderthal type with a very low forehead? You can't always count on having high, smooth, white brows, you know, like Luke's.'

'Try not to be facetious, darling, it's quite serious. Then I put their jewels into dainty little chintz bags made out of Fortmason remnants.'

'When you say you do all this, what exactly do you mean?'

'Well, darling, I should do it if there was a raid. It's rather like private theatricals, you know what I mean. "It'll be all right on the night" kind of idea. The worse the dress rehearsal, the better the show, and so on.'

Mary became very scornful and said it was the stupidest job she had ever heard of. 'Jewels,' she said, 'in chintz bags. Writing M and F. Really, Sophia, I give up.'

Sophia said it was better than doing nothing like Mary, and they rang off, each in a huff.

When Sophia saw Rudolph she said she had heard that he had been seen out with a duck-billed platypus disguised as a Sultana. (Olga's rather long, turned-up nose was considered to be one of her great attractions.)

'Yes, my little Puss-puss,' he said, 'I did take the alluring Princess to a movie what time you went whoring round with your Cabinet puddings.'

'I thought you told me you were going to play bridge at your club?'

'So I was, until I met Olga.'

'But where did you meet her?'

'At my club.'

'Rudolph, what a story.'

'Well, I did. She came along in a taxi after I had telephoned to her.'

'Oh. What was she like?'

'Cracking bore, as usual. Talked about nothing but herself. I had to hear the whole story of how Serge blighted her life by refusing to allow her self-expression on the films. As though one didn't know that the old boyar would allow her to do anything which brought in the roubles.'

'She was always having tests,' said Sophia.

'And they were lousy. Well, then of course she is having all those books dedicated to her and pictures painted of her, and so on. But she has abandoned these activities for a very important job under the Government. First Aid Post, I guess. Chap in my club, a doctor, gave her her first aid exam. He said, "Now Princess, if you found a man with a badly broken leg and you had no splint or bandage, what would you do?' and she said, "Take my drawers off and tie the leg to my leg." So of course he passed her.'

Sophia saw that she must look out. She knew very well that when a man is thoroughly disloyal about a woman, and at the same time begins to indulge in her company, he nearly always intends to have an affair with that woman. The disloyalty is in itself a danger signal. She would not have supposed that Olga was exactly to Rudolph's taste, but these things do not follow any known rules and you never can tell.

'Beastly fellow,' she said. 'I see you're in love with her.'

'Rather,' said Rudolph. 'I see you're jealous.'

'Rather.' Sophia got up and rang the bell for the cocktail things. 'I say, darling, by the way, you know Florence?'

'Yes, I'm in love with her too, of course?'

'Very likely. Anyhow, you know she lives with us now. Well, I believe she must be nicer than we thought she was, because, whatever do you think? She keeps a pigeon in her bedroom.'

'Does she now? I thought she kept Luke.'

'No, no, darling, I've often told you. Anyway, there it is, she keeps this terribly nice pigeon.'

'Whatever for?'

'I expect it is her friend. I would love to have a sweet pigeon for a friend, but I must say I never would have thought it of Florence, she doesn't strike one as an animal lover. Milly doesn't like her at all.'

'I call it very queer,' said Rudolph. 'Do you think it might have some religious significance?'

'It's a pigeon, not a dove.'

'Florence wouldn't know the difference. That's it, I

expect she is keeping it to let loose over Brother Bones's head next time she sees him.'

'Or maybe she saved its life. Mr. Stone, in our Post, you know, has to keep down the London pigeons in peace time, and he says it's awfully difficult because wherever you put your trap some old lady always pops her head out of a window and sets up a screeching about it and calls in the police and so on. However early in the morning, it's always just the same. So the result is that London's pigeons are not really kept down very much, as you may note. Perhaps Florence saw this one in a trap (they get up very early in the Brotherhood, you know), and promised not to let it loose again if she might have it. I like her much better for it, actually.'

Florence now came into the room. She told Sophia that Luke had been guided to ask a hundred people to dinner the next day to talk about Moral Rearmament. 'It's to meet this friend of ours, Heatherley Egg,' she said. (Florence always introduced new people into her conversation with the word 'this'. 'This woman I met in the bus' or 'This cousin of my father's'. It was a habit which maddened Sophia.) 'I have arranged the whole thing,' Florence continued; 'gold chairs and food and so on are all ordered. I just looked in here to say how much we hope you will come to it, as I feel sure you will be interested. Heatherley Egg has just arrived from the States, and he will tell us what the President said to him about Moral Rearmament. Just the two of them (the three, I should say, because of course, there was a Third present) talked it over for nearly five minutes, and Heth

41

says—well, you must hear it from his own lips to-morrow evening. There will be members of the Brother-hood from all, yes, I am happy to say, all the European countries.'

Sophia and Rudolph hurriedly explained that they had a very long-standing engagement for the following evening. Florence looked a bit crucified and said how strange it must seem to live in a perpetual whirl of thoughtless gaiety.

'I call a hundred people to dinner a pretty good whirl, personally. '

Florence said she must go as she had this First Aid lecture.

'It was her book I saw that awful old knee joint in.'

Sophia went to the telephone and dialled a number. 'You know I really admire her for doing the first aid course, I never would have expected it, like the pigeon, and dyeing her hair. It all shows how I underestimated Florence.' She rang up Vocal Lodge and asked Sir Ivor whether she and Rudolph might dine with him the next day. 'There is a Brotherhood orgy here, and we can't take it.'

'Yes, Sophie, my darling, you may, but you must be nice to the Gogothskys who are coming, and not make poor dear Olga cry like you did last time. Promise? All right, eight o'clock then, I have to be at my post by ten.'

'Thank goodness for that,' said Sophia to Rudolph when she had rung off. 'People from every European country, think of it. I mean the whole point of the war is one doesn't have to see foreigners any more. And as for what the President said to Heth—horrors!'

42

The Russians marched into Poland on the very day of Florence's party. Luke was stunned by this practical demonstration of Russo-German solidarity.

'Herr Hitler told me himself that his life's work was to lead a crusade against Bolshevism.'

'Then you ought to have smelt a rat at once,' said Sophia unkindly.

'But he was so earnest about it. He said over and over again that Bolshevism was the greatest force for evil the world has ever known.'

'Of course I don't want to say I told you so, darling, but there's never been a pin to put between the Communists and the Nazis. The Communists torture you to death if you're not a worker, and the Nazis torture you to death if you're not a German. If you are they look at your nose first. Aristocrats are inclined to prefer Nazis while Jews prefer Bolshies. An old bourgeois like yourself, Luke, should keep your fingers out of both their pies.'

Luke must have been quite distracted. He did not even protest, as he usually did, when Sophia called him a bourgeois, that the Garfields were an old Saxon family dating back to before the Conquest. Which, as Sophia would very justly observe, did not affect the matter one way or another.

'And let me tell you,' she went on, 'if you continue to believe everything those foreigners in Germany said to you, you are in for some very nasty shocks, old boy. They have told a lot of people a lot of things not strictly speaking true, and most of us are beginning to get wise. The day they said they would never use gas against

43

civilians every First Aid Post in London let down
its gas-proof flaps, and we have all stifled ever
since.'

Poor Luke passed his hand over his smooth, white
forehead and looked sad. Sophia was sorry that she had
been so beastly to him, and said, 'Darling, are you
excited for your party to-night?'

'I am not a baby to be excited for a party. It will, I
hope, be interesting. Mr. Egg appears to have seen the
President.'

So Rudolph was right, and Luke was getting bored
with the Brotherhood. She wondered whether it was a
religion which took a great hold on people, and whether
it would leave the poor fellow with an uneasy con-
science for the rest of his life.

Brothers and Sisters now began flocking into the
house. They all looked very much alike and might
easily, had there not been a hundred of them, have been
brothers and sisters indeed. The girls were all dressed
in simple little tub frocks with a bastard Tyrolean
flavour, they wore no hats or stockings, and quite a lot
of grimy toes poked their way out of sandals. They were
sunburnt, their foreheads were wrinkled, and their hair
and lips were very thin. The young men, of whom there
were quantities, appeared at first sight to be extremely
well dressed, but their suits were too broad at the
shoulder, too slim in the hips, and not made of quite
the very best stuff—in fact, they would not stand up to
close examination. They answered to names like Heth
for Heatherley, Ken for Kennerley, and Win for Winthrop, and spoke with Hollywood accents. They were

sunburnt, and when you first looked at them, immensely handsome, like the suits. Their eyes and teeth were blue. The cosmopolitan element in this party was not in evidence, and Sophia thought Florence must have meant Americans from every country in Europe, until she heard a gabble of foreign languages. She concluded that the Brotherhood, like Hollywood, places its own stamp on all nationalities, as it certainly confers a particular type of looks, of clothes, and that 'If this is pleasure give me pain' expression which is permanently on all the faces of its adherents. There was not one soul in uniform.

Rudolph, however, when he arrived to take Sophia down to Kew was resplendent in the full fig of the Wessex Guards.

'I kept it secret for a surprise for you,' he said; 'wait till you see my coat, though, lined with scarlet.'

'Well, you do look pretty,' said Sophia approvingly. Before the war, she had often thought of seeing him in uniform for the first time, and had supposed that she would cry. Now she simply felt delighted. Indeed Rudolph, unusually well shaved, looked handsome and soldierly, an example, she felt, to the brothers. War psychology, so incomprehensible during peace time, already had her in its grip.

Florence introduced Mr. Egg to them. 'Heatherley, this is Sophia Garfield. Rudolph, this is Heatherley.' Brotherhood manners were like that. 'Sophia, you must wait a moment while Heth tells us what the President said to him. He's just going to now.' She got up on a chair and clapped her hands. 'Silence everybody,

45

please. Heatherley is going to tell us what the President said about Moral Rearmament.'

Silence fell at once, and all faces were turned towards Heatherley who was scrambling on to the chair.

'Well, folks,' he said impressively, 'I went to see the President.' Pause. 'We were alone together, just the three of us, you understand. The President is a busy man.' Pause. 'Well, he said to me.' An impressive pause. Heatherley looked all round the room, and finally continued, 'He said "I think Moral Rearmament is a very very fine idea."'

There was a prolonged and reverent silence, broken by Florence who said, 'I always think it is so important to hear the exact words when a man like that makes a statement like that. Thank you, Heth; personally I shall treasure this little scene.'

The Gogothskys were already at Vocal Lodge when Sophia and Rudolph arrived. Olga, greatly to Sophia's delight, for she made a mental collection of Olga's clothes, was wearing a snood. A bit of it came round and fastened under her chin like a beard and she looked, as no doubt she felt, very Slav. The Prince, a huge jolly drunken fellow whom everybody liked, was dressed in Air Force blue; he announced that he was on leave from his balloon, Blossom. It was evident that Blossom had made a man of him. Hitherto his life had been spent trailing about after Olga, making, in return for her considerable income, the small and rather unreal (as he was a British subject), but in his wife's eyes, invaluable, contribution of princedom. Now he was

46

bronzed, clean, fairly well shaven, and apparently quite sober. He and Rudolph slapped each other on the back, compared uniforms and were very gay.

'You managed to get away from your Chief,' Sophia said to Olga, her eyes feasting on the snood.

'He heard of my sorrow and begged me to take some leave,' said Olga reproachfully.

'Sorrow?' said Rudolph. 'Why, you are looking a bit widowed, come to think of it. What's up?'

'My relations in Poland——'

'Didn't know you had any,' said Sophia sceptically.

'Didn't you, darling? Yes, indeed, my great-great-great-grandmother was a Paczinska, and I fear my poor cousins must have fallen into Bolshevik hands. You know what that meant in Russia—they were given over to their peasantry to do as they liked with.' Olga gave a tremendous shudder.

Sophia said there must be something wrong somewhere. If the Duchess of Devonshire, for instance, was handed over to the peasantry to do as they liked with, they would no doubt put her in the best bedroom and get her a cup of tea. 'If the peasantry are really such demons,' she said, 'whose fault is that, pray?'

'But I saw in the papers that the Bolshies are going in on purpose to protect you White Russians,' said old Ivor, rather puzzled.

Serge Gogothsky had been brought up in England, and had spent most of his life here. He must, therefore, have been well accustomed to the national ignorance on the subject of foreign affairs, but this was too much even for him. He gave a sort of warbling roar, and

47

jumped about the room like an agonized Petrushka explaining the historical and geographical position of White Russia.

'All right, keep your hair on,' said the old singer, taking his off and adjusting a curl. 'Have another drink.'

This panacea for all ills was accepted, and peace reigned once more until Rudolph tactlessly observed that he was not so enthusiastic about Europe being over-run by the murderous Muscovites as Hitler seemed to be. The Prince once more became very much excited, and said that if the Allies had assisted the White Russians at the end of the last war and enabled them to reinstate the Romanoffs, none of this would have happened.

'What nonsense. The Romanoffs were just as likely to get imperial ideas as Uncle Joe any day of the week. You Asiatics should be kept out of Europe, that's what it is.'

'Keep your hairs on, dears, and let's have dinner,' said Sir Ivor, who only enjoyed joking conversations of an esoteric kind.

During dinner Sophia noticed that Olga was droop-ing her eyelids a good deal at Rudolph who seemed not to be disliking it. She cast about for means of retaliation (upon Rudolph, Olga she could always deal with very easily) but saw none to hand. The old gentleman would hardly bring conviction as a stalking horse, and the trouble with Serge was that the smallest encourage-ment too often led to rape. A tremendous dip of the offending eyelids stung Sophia into action and she turned to Olga with a sweet smile and asked how Savonarola was getting along. She always reserved this question for very special occasions.

'Dearest, there is a war on, you know. Sometimes, however, I do manage to do a little scribbling, busy as I am my poetry simply forces its way on to paper. Last night, during a lull, I read some of my sonnets to the Chief. He says they remind him of Elizabeth Browning's Sonnets to the Portuguese.'

'From,' said Rudolph. 'Who is your Chief?'

Olga gave a great swoop of the eyelids, and said that her job, which was very important, and her Chief, who was very very famous, had to be kept very very secret.

'Bet Haw-haw knows them,' said Rudolph. 'I suppose you are one of those pin-money lovelies I am always reading about, eh? Come clean now, aren't you?'

'By the way, dears, I have a new job,' said Ivor.

Sophia wrestled with temptation. She longed to take Olga down a peg by being in the know; the old gentleman was just going to tell them himself, so where would be the harm? On the other hand, Fred had begged her to be careful. She decided to wait and see what Ivor said. Meanwhile the conversation flowed on.

Rudolph said, 'I suppose you are a wonderful old spy in a wonderful new wig. I suppose that's what Olga is really, a beautiful female spy, worming her way into the hearts of careless young officers like Serge and me.' Olga, who liked to be taken very seriously, was not pleased. She drooped her eyelids at the Empire *dessus de table* instead of at Rudolph, and Sophia relaxed once more.

'Talking of jobs, you should see Sophia's Post,' went on Rudolph, who, entirely against her orders, was always popping in and out of it. 'Serge, old boy, here's a tip for you—the first thing that strikes the eye is a notice, written out in wobbling capitals by our Sophia, which says, "Never give a drink to a patient marked H." See the form, you old mujik, the great thing is never by any chance let yourself be marked H. Farther on, however, you come to notices with arrows attached, also written by our little friend, and therefore extremely unprofessional in appearance, saying, "Males remove underclothing here", "Females remove underclothing here", and these lead, quite logically, to the midwifery department. I had no idea the Borough Councils were such realists.'

'It's called the Labour Ward,' said Sophia; 'don't listen to him, he has no business to come prying round my Post.'

'The Labour Ward has to be seen to be believed,' said Rudolph; 'it's a kind of dog kennel, and the only furnishings are a cradle and a pair of woolly boots. If I were a lady I should bag not having a baby there, I must say, raid or no raid.'

'Poor Sister Wordsworth can't get anybody to take charge of it, did I tell you?' said Sophia, falling happily into talking shop. 'You see, it's awfully dull just sitting and looking at the cradle all day, they prefer the treatment room.'

'But the real thrill is the Hospital Museum,' went on

Rudolph. 'It's next door to the Labour Ward—very suitable really, as exhibit A is a bottle containing pre-natal Siamese twins. You should come along one day, Serge, and take a load of the ulcerated stomachs. I promise nobody shall mark you H, and there's a pub up the street.'

'You've none of you taken any interest in my new job,' said the King of Song peevishly.

'Darling Ivor, how beastly of us. Come clean, then. What is it?'

'I'm to go down to Torquay with our evacuated orchids.'

Chapter Four

SOPHIA sat by her telephone at the Post, and tried not to long for an air raid. On the one or two occasions when she had lifted up the receiver and had heard, instead of the Medical Officer of Health wishing to speak to Sister Wordsworth, 'This is the Southern Report Centre. Air raid warning Yellow,' she had experienced such an unhealthy glow of excitement that she felt she might easily become a raid addict, or take to raids in the same way that people do to drugs, and for much the same reason. Her life outside the Post had ceased to be much fun, for Rudolph, after looking almost too pretty in his uniform for about a week, was now paying the penalty attached to such prettiness in a training camp on the East Coast.

Inside the Post she made up things to keep her occupied, as people do who lie for weeks in bed not particularly ill. She looked a great deal at her watch, knitted, read Macaulay's *History of England*, wrote quantities of unnecessary letters for the first time since she was a girl, and chatted to Sister Wordsworth. Finally, as a last resort, there was the wireless. Sophia hated the wireless. It seemed to her to be a definite and living force for evil in the land. When she turned it on, she thought of the women all over England in lonely little houses with their husbands gone to the war, sick with anxiety for the future. She saw them putting their children to bed, their

52

hearts broken by the loneliness of the evening hours, and then, for company, turning on the wireless. What is the inspiration which flows to them from this, the fountain-head, as it must seem to them, of the Empire? London, with all its resources of genius, talent, wit, how does London help them through these difficult times? How are they made to feel that England is not only worth dying for but being poor for, being lonely and unhappy for? With great music, stirring words and sound common sense? With the glorious literature, nobly spoken, of our ancestors? Not at all. With facetiousness and jazz.

Chatting to Sister Wordsworth was her favourite occupation. This young and pretty creature turned out to be a remarkable person in many ways. Before the war, she had been a health visitor, and Sophia, who knew but little of such matters, discovered that this was a profession which required the combination of a really impressive training with such virtues as tact, knowledge of human nature, sense of humour, and a complete lack of pretentiousness. Sister Wordsworth's charming, rather hearty manner was that of a schoolgirl, decep-tively young, but she was a nurse, certified midwife, and trained psychologist, and furthermore, had an extensive knowledge of law. Week after week she kept close upon a hundred idle people in that Post contented, on good terms with each other, and in so far as she could invent things for them to do, busy. Of course, there were troubles and difficulties. A German Jew had come to the Post as a voluntary worker; after two days the nurses had sent a deputation to Sister Wordsworth saying that they could not work in the same building as a Prussian spy, and she was obliged to send him to the next Post in the district where it was to be hoped that a more tolerant spirit prevailed. Sophia had been greatly tickled by this, and had wished that a few Prussians could have had a look at their prototype. She asked why he was supposed to be a spy. It seemed that he had spent half an hour reading the notices which were displayed everywhere in the Post, and which pertained to such things as the horrid fate of patients marked H, hot-water-bottles to be filled at certain specified hours, the quantity of sterilized instruments to be kept handy, and so on. Sophia, who had written most of them out herself, could not believe that the High Command in Berlin would find its path greatly smoothed by such information. Still, as Fred had remarked when she told him about it, 'You can't be too careful, and after all, we are at war with the Germans.' Fred had a wonderful way of hitting nails on the head.

To-day it was a Sunday, and all was very quiet in the Post. Sister Wordsworth was out, the wireless programme absolutely impossible, and the workmen who generally made life hideous with their bangings were able, unlike the personnel of the Post, to take Sundays off. Sophia did her knitting. She was a bad, slow knitter, and the sleeves of anything she made were always too short. She listened dreamily to a conversation which was going on beyond the sacking partition. Three of the nurses were discussing a certain foreign Royal Family with an inaccuracy astonishing as to every detail. It all sounded rather cosy and delicious, and Sophia would have liked to join in. One of the penalties, however, attached to immunity from knee-joints was that she was incarcerated in the office. The people in the treatment room had lovely gossips, but the day would come when they would have knees as well; in order to avoid the knees, she was obliged to forgo the gossips.

'St. Anne's Hospital First Aid Post

'Darling, darling, darling, darling,
'I say, Florence's bird is house-trained, I saw her letting it out of the window like a dog last thing at night. I only saw this because I happened to be in that loo which isn't blacked out, with the light off, of course, and I heard a great flapping and Florence's window opening, so I was guided to look out. As there is a moon, I saw it quite clearly streaking off to do its business with a most determined look on its face. I waited for ages, but it didn't come back. What d'you suppose it does, peck on the window, or coo or what? Well, I should love to have a terribly nice, pretty faithful house-trained pigeon, what with missing Mily and so on, and I said so this morning to Florence, but she gave me a simply horrid look, so perhaps she thought I was laughing at her or something which indeed I wasn't. Really I am getting quite attached to Florence, and it's nice for Luke having her around, with me here such a lot, gives him something else to think about besides the Income Tax. Poor old thing, he looks fearfully tucked up about that, and of course it must be hell paying all those seven and sixes for a

55

war you don't believe in much. Besides, he feels quite torn in two between his heroes, Our Premier and Herr Hitler, now they don't tread the same path any longer.

'Darling, how is camp life, and do you miss me? Florence quite misses you, you know, perhaps she is in love with you. She keeps on coming into my room to ask what your address is, and what battalion you have joined, and how long you will be training, and who your commanding officer is and all sorts of things. I expect you'll get a balaclava for Christmas; she is knitting one for some lucky fellow, but I think he must be one of those African pigmies with a top knot by the shape of it.

'Oh dear, I do love you, love from your darling
'SOPHIA.

'PS. Olga is really putting on a most peculiar act. She lunched alone at the Ritz yesterday in a black wig, a battle bowler and her sables, and pretended not to know any of her friends. Half-way through lunch a page-boy (she had bribed him no doubt) brought her a note, and she gave a sort of shriek, put a veil over the whole thing, battle bowler and all, and scrammed. So now of course everyone knows for certain she is a beautiful female spy. Poor old Serge has been dismissed his Blossom because he passed out and so did it; I hear they looked too indecent lying side by side in the Park.'

As Sophia finished her letter Sister Wordsworth came in.

'Oh, Lady Sophia,' she said, 'I forgot to tell you that

a friend of yours came to see me yesterday morning. She is joining the Post to-morrow for the night shift, full time. It is lucky as we are so very short-handed on that shift.'

'A friend of mine—what's she called?'

'Miss—I have it written down here, wait a minute— oh, yes, Miss Turnbull.'

'Gracious,' said Sophia, 'you surprise me. I never would have thought it of Florence. She hasn't said a word about it to me. Can I go now?'

'Yes, do. I shall be here the whole evening.'

Sophia found herself, for the first time since the beginning of the war, dining alone with Luke. It struck her that he wanted to have an intimate conversation with her, but did not quite know how to begin. Sophia would have been willing to help him; she was feeling quite soft towards Luke these days, he looked so ill and unhappy, but intimate conversations, except very occasionally with Rudolph, were not much in her line.

Luke began by saying that he was going back to the Foreign Office.

'How about your business?'

'There isn't any,' he said shortly, 'and I must tell you, my dear Sophia, that you and I are going to be very much poorer.'

'So I supposed. Well, you must decide what we ought to do. We could move into the garage at the back of the house very easily, and I could manage with a daily maid, or none at all. I should probably have to work shorter hours at the Post in that case.'

57

Luke, who was always put out by Sophia's apparent indifference to the advantages his money had brought her, shook his head impatiently. 'We shall be forced to make various radical economies by the very fact of there being a war. I shall not travel as I used to, we shall not entertain, there will be no question of any shooting or fishing, and you I presume will not be wanting much in the way of new clothes. There is absolutely no need to reduce our standard of living any further for the present. Besides, I should think it very wrong to send away any servants.'

'Except Greta,' said Sophia. 'I wish to goodness we could get rid of her. I simply hate having a German about the place, and so do the others. Mrs. Round keeps on saying to me, "Not to be able to talk world politics in one's own servants' hall is very upsetting for all of us." I'm sure it must be. And yet I haven't the heart to put her in the street, poor thing. It's all my own fault, I never liked her but I was too lazy to give her notice, you know how it is.'

'Better keep her on for a time, now she is here.'

'Oh yes, I know. We must really.'

They ate on in a polite and not very comfortable silence.

Luke said presently, 'Sophia, I hope you don't object to Florence staying on here.'

'Of course not.'

'She is very poor, you know. I don't know what would become of her unless we could help her.'

Sophia's eyebrows went up. She thought that the Brotherhood must really be improving Luke's character. Hitherto he had despised, disliked and mistrusted people for no better reason than that they were poor.

'Well then, of course we must help her,' she said warmly. 'I wonder—perhaps she would think it awful cheek if I offered to give her my silver-fox coat. I never wear it now, and I know they are not fashionable, but it is extremely warm.'

'That is very good of you, my dear Sophia, and I am sure if you were guided to share it with her she would be only too happy to accept.'

Sophia stifled the temptation to say that she would arrange for it to come clean at Sketchley's first.

'I'm very glad Florence is here to keep you company when I'm at the Post,' she said; 'actually she has joined the Post too now, did you know, but our shifts only overlap by about an hour. It's really very good of her; she is going to do a twelve-hour night shift, simply horrible I should think.'

'Florence is, of course, one of the people who believed, as I did, that Herr Hitler and Our Premier between them could make a very wonderful thing of world relationships. Like me, she is bitterly disillusioned by Herr Hitler's treacherous (yes, it is the only word) treacherous behaviour to Our Premier. But like me, she feels that this cruel war is not the proper solution, it can only cause a deterioration in world affairs and will settle nothing. People who think as we do are ploughing a lone furrow just now, you know, Sophia.'

'What I can't see is why you think that the behaviour of the Germans has been any worse, or different, during the past few months from what it always is. Anybody who can read print knows what they are like, cruel and treacherous, they have always been the same since the days of the Roman Empire. I can't see why we have to wait for Government Blue Books and White Papers to tell us all this—oh well,' she said, 'what's the good of talking about it now? I really do feel awfully sorry for you, Luke, as you have so many friends over there and thought everything was going to be rosy.'

'Don't misunderstand me,' said Luke, earnestly, 'I consider that Herr Hitler has treated Our Premier most outrageously. At the same time, I feel that if the British people had gone all out for moral rearmament and real appeasement, things need never have reached this pass.'

'The British people indeed, that's a good one, I must say. However, it's now quite obvious to any thinking man that our lot in life is to fight the huns about once in every twenty years. I'm beginning to consider having a baby; we shall need all we can muster to cope with the 1942 class in 1960, who, if there is anything in heredity, will be the most awful brutes.'

Luke, who belonged to the 'We have no quarrel with the German people' school of thought, looked wistful, and presently went off to his smoking-room.

Rudolph wrote:

'It is exactly like one's private here. One of the masters gave us bayonet drill this morning—this is how it goes:

' "The first thing we 'ave got to consider is wot are the parts of a soldier? First you 'ave the 'ead. Now, the 'ead of a soldier is covered with a tin 'at, so it ain't of no good to go sloshing it with a bay'net becos all yer gits is a rattle. Wot ave we next—the throat, and the throat is a very different proposition. Two inches of bay'net there, and yer gits the wind-pipe and the jugular. Very good. Next we comes to wot yer might call the united dairies. A soldier's dairies are well covered with ammunition pouches and for this reason should be left alone, and also becos a very little lower down yer gits the belly. Now it only requires three inches of bayonet in the belly, twist it well, and out they comes, liver and lights and all. Etc. (I spare you the rest of the anatomical analysis.) Now, when pursuing a retreating enemy, you should always make a jab for 'is kidneys becos it will then go in like butter and come out like butter. When the —— is wounded, you should kneel on 'is chest and bash his face with the butt end, thus keeping the bay'net ready in case you want it to jab at some other —— with. You've got to 'ate the ——s or yer won't git nowhere with them." (Tremendous pantomime.) If it wasn't so heavenly, I might easily have felt sick.

'How are you? If you ask me, I think Florence is more of a beautiful female spy than Olga; I call all this bird-life extremely suspicious. I shall be having some leave soon and intend to conduct a rigid investigation in Flossie's bedroom. Meanwhile you be on the look-out for suspicious behaviour—cameras, for instance, people lurking on the stairs, false bottoms to trunks and all the other paraphernalia.

'I don't get along without you very well.

'Love and xxxx Rudolph.'

Chapter Five

THE newspapers suddenly awoke from the wartime hibernation and were able to splash their pages with a story which all their readers could enjoy. The idol of the British people, the envy of all civilized nations, the hero of a thousand programmes, The Grand Old Gentleman of Vocal Lodge, in short none other than the famous King of Song, Sir Ivor King himself, had been found brutally done to death in the Pagoda at Kew Gardens. Here was a tale to arouse interest in the bosoms of all but the most hardened cynics, and indeed the poor old man's compatriots, as they chewed their bacon and eggs the following morning, were convulsed with rather delicious shudders. The naked corpse, they learnt, surmounted by that beloved old bald head, had been mutilated and battered with instruments ranging from the bluntness of a croquet mallet to the sharpness of a butcher's knife. This treatment had rendered the face unrecognizable, and only the cranium had been left untouched. His clothes had been removed and there was no trace of them, but his favourite wig, dishevelled and bloodstained, was found, late in the evening, by two little children innocently playing on Kew Green. Those lucky ones among the breakfasting citizens who subscribed to the *Daily Runner* began their day with

WIGLESS HEAD ON KEW PAGODA, HEADLESS WIG ON GREEN

Later, when they issued forth into the streets it was to find that the placards of the evening papers had entirely abandoned 'U-Boat Believed Sunk', 'Nazi Planes Believed Down', 'Hitler's Demands', 'Stalin's Demands', and the reactions of the U.S.A., and were devoting themselves to what soon became known as the Wig Outrage. 'Wig on Green Sensation, Latest.' 'Pagoda Corpse—Foul Play?' 'Wig Mystery, Police Baffled.'

When the inquest was held, the police were obliged to issue an appeal to the great crowds that were expected, begging them to stay at home in view of the target which they would present to enemy bombers. In spite of this warning, the Wig Inquest was all too well attended, and the Wig Coroner had a few words to say about this generation's love of the horrible. Indeed, Chiswick High Road had the aspect of Epsom Heath at Derby Day's most scintillating moment.

It would be difficult to do better, for an account of the Wig Inquest than to switch over, as they say on the wireless, to the columns of the *Evening Runner*:

INQUEST ON WIG MURDER
VALET'S STATEMENT
ONLY CURLED LAST WEEK
WAS MURDERED MAN THE KING OF SONG?

'The "colonel's lady and Judy O'Grady" fought for places at the inquest to-day on the body, which was

63

found last Friday in Kew Pagoda, and which is presumed to be that of Sir Ivor King, "the King of Song". The body was so extensively mutilated that a formal identification was impossible, although Mr. Larch, Sir Ivor's valet, swore that he would recognize that particular cranium anywhere as belonging to the "King".

'His Master's Voice

'Giving evidence, Mr. Larch, who showed signs of great emotion, said that Sir Ivor had left Vocal Lodge to go up to London at two o'clock on Friday afternoon. He had seemed rather nervous and said that he had to keep a very important appointment in town, but that he would be back in time to change for a local sing-song he had promised to attend after tea. His master's voice, said Mr. Larch, had been in great demand with A.R.P. organizations, and Mr. Larch thought that what with so much singing, and the evacuations in the Orchid House, Sir Ivor had been looking strained and tired of late. By tea-time he had not returned. Mr. Larch did not feel unduly worried. "Sir Ivor had the temperament of an artiste, and was both unpunctual and vague, sometimes spending whole nights in the Turkish bath without informing his staff that he intended to sleep out."

'His Favourite Wig

' "When the children brought in the wig," went on Mr. Larch, "I thought it was eerie, as it was his favourite wig; we only had it curled last week, and he would never have thrown it away. Besides, I knew he had no spare with him. I immediately notified the police.'' Here Mr. Larch broke down and had to be assisted out of the court.

'Mr. Smith, taxi-driver, said that the old person first of all told him to go to the Ritz, but stopped him at Turnham Green and was driven back to the gates of Kew Gardens where he paid the fare, remarking that it was a fine day for a walk. He was singing loudly in a deep tenor all the while, and seemed in excellent spirits.

'A Very High Note

'Mr. Jumont, a gardener at Kew Gardens, said that he was manuring the rhododendrons when he heard the "King" go past on a very high note.

'The Coroner: "Did you see him?"

'Mr. Jumont: "No, sir. But there was no mistaking that old party when he was singing soprano. Besides, this was his favourite song, 'When I am dead, my dearest'." (Music by the Marchioness of Waterford.)

'At these words there was a sensation, and hardly a dry eye in court. Some fashionably dressed ladies were sobbing so loudly that the Coroner threatened to have them evicted unless they could control themselves.

'Continuing his evidence, Mr. Jumont said that Sir Ivor seemed to be walking in the direction of the Pagoda, the time being about 3 p.m.

'A Wonderful Thatch

'Mr. Bott, another employee at Kew Gardens, told how he had found the body. Just before closing time he

65

noticed some blood stains and one or two blond curls at the foot of the Pagoda, then saw that the Pagoda door, which is always kept locked, stood ajar. He went in, and a trail of blood on the stairs led him to the very top where the sight which met his eyes was so terrible that he nearly swooned. "More like a butcher's shop it was, and it gave me a nasty turn."

'Coroner: "Did it seem to you at the time that this might be the body of Sir Ivor King?"

'Mr. Bott: "No, sir. For one thing the old gentleman (who, of course, I knew very well by sight) always seemed to have a wonderful thatch, as you might say, for his age, but the only thing I could clearly see about the individual on the Pagoda was that he hadn't a hair to his name."

'Mr. Bott said, in answer to further questioning, that it had never occurred to him Sir Ivor King's hair might have been a wig.

'One or two more witnesses having been examined, the Coroner's jury, without retiring, returned a verdict of murder by person or persons unknown.

'The Coroner said there was an overwhelming presumption that the corpse was that of Sir Ivor King.'

Next day, the *Daily Runner*, in its column of pocket leading articles called BRITAIN EXPECTS, in which what Britain generally Expects is a new Minister for Agriculture, had a short paragraph headed:

'MOURN THE KING OF SONG

'A very gallant and loved old figure has gone from

our midst. Mourn him. But remember that he now belongs to the past. It is our duty to say that in the circumstances of his death there may be more than meets the eye. One of our Cabinet Ministers may be guilty of negligence. If so, we should like to see a statement made in Parliament.

'*Our* grief must not blind us to *his* fault. For remember that *we* belong to the future.'

There was more than met the eye. Sure enough, the very next day it was learned from reliable sources that the King of Song had been a trump-card in the hand of the Government. He had, in fact, been about to inaugurate, in conjunction with the B.B.C., Ministry of Information, and Foreign Office, the most formidible campaign of Propaganda through the medium of Song that the world has ever seen. The British and French Governments, not only they, but democrats everywhere, had attached great importance to the scheme. They had estimated that it would have a profound effect upon neutral opinion, and indeed might well bring America into the war, on one side or another. Without the King of Song to lead it, this campaign would fall as flat as a pancake, no other living man or woman having the requisite personality or range of voice to conduct it. It must, therefore, necessarily be abandoned. Thus his untimely and gruesome end constituted about as severe a blow to the Allied cause as the loss of a major engagement would have done.

The horrid word Sabotage, the even horrider word Leakage, were now breathed, and poor Fred, who was given no credit for having conceived the idea, was universally execrated for not having delivered it. In the same way that the First Lord of the Admiralty is held responsible for the loss of a capital ship, so the death of Sir Ivor was laid at poor Fred's door. He made a statement in the House that mollified nobody, and Britain Expected every morning that he would resign. Britain did not expect it more than poor Fred expected that he would have to; however, in the end he got off with a nasty half-hour at No. 10. It was now supposed that the King of Song had been liquidated by German spies who had fallen into Kew Gardens in parachutes, and Sophia said 'I told you so' to Luke, and hardly dared look out of her bedroom window any more.

Sophia was really upset by the whole business. She had loved her old godfather, and having always seen a great deal of him she would miss him very much. On the other hand, it cannot be denied that she found a certain element of excitement in her near connection with so ghastly and so famous a murder—especially when, the day after the inquest, Sir Ivor's solicitor rang her up and told her, very confidentially, that Vocal Lodge and everything in it had been left to her. She had also inherited a substantial fortune and a jet tiara.

Sophia now considered herself entitled to assume the gratifying rôle of mourner in chief. She took a day off from the Post, instructed Rawlings to fill up the car with a month's ration of petrol, and drove round to the Brompton Oratory. Here she spent an hour with a high dignitary of the Roman Church arranging for a Requiem Mass to be held at the Oratory. The dignitary was such a charmer, and Sophia was so conscious of looking extremely pretty in her new black hat, that she cast about for ways of prolonging the interview. Finally she handed over a large sum of money so that masses could be sung in perpetuity for the old gentleman's soul; and when she remembered the eternal basting to which he had so recently condemned her, she considered that this was a high-minded and generous deed on her part. This transaction over, she made great efforts to edge the conversation round to her own soul, but the dignitary, unlike Florence, seemed completely uninterested in so personal a subject, and very soon, with tact and charm but great firmness, indicated to her that she might go. Sophia, as she drove away, reflected that whatever you might say about Popery it is, at least, a professional religion, and shows up to a great advantage when compared with such mushroom growths as the Boston Brotherhood.

On her way to Vocal Lodge she went to pick up Lady Beech who had consented to accompany her on her sad pilgrimage. She was to meet the solicitor there, see Sir Ivor's servants and make various arrangements connected with her legacy. Lady Beech lived in Kensington Square. She was evidently determined to take the fullest advantage of Sophia's petrol ration, for, when the car drew up at her front door, she was already standing on the steps beside an enormous object of no particular shape done up in sacking.

'Very late,' she said. 'Most unlike you. I know, darling, that you won't mind taking this little bed to Heal's on our way.'

This rather delayed matters. It became evident, during the course of the drive, that Lady Beech very much wished that Vocal Lodge had been left to her instead of to Sophia.

'Oh, darling, what a pity,' said Sophia; 'silly old gentleman not to think of it. Of course I'm going to give it to the Nation, don't you think that's right, really? To be kept exactly as it is, a Shrine of Song, and I am giving some of the money he left to keep it up. He left nearly a quarter of a million, you know, so I am going to build an Ivor King Home of Rest for aged singers, and an Ivor King Concert Hall as well. Don't you think he'd be pleased?'

'Very wonderful of you, my dear,' said Lady Beech gloomily. 'Tell me, now, had it occurred to you what a very much more interesting gift to the Nation Vocal Lodge would be if somebody lived in it—I mean somebody rather cultivated, with rather exquisite taste? She could preserve the spirit of the place, don't you see? Like those châteaux on the Loire which have their original families living in them.'

Sophia said she had just the very person in mind, an old governess of her own, who was extremely cultivated and had perfectly exquisite taste. Lady Beech sighed deeply.

When they arrived at Vocal Lodge, Sophia was closeted for some time, first with the solicitor and then with Sir Ivor's servants, whom she begged to stay on there for the rest of their lives if it suited them. Larch took her upstairs and showed her all Sir Ivor's wigs laid out on his bed, rather as it might have been a pilgrimage

70

to view the body. He was evidently, like Sophia, divided between genuine sorrow and a feeling of self-importance.

'The Press, m'lady,' he said with relish, 'awful they've been. Nosing round everywhere and taking photos. And the lies they tell, I don't know if you saw, m'lady, they said cook had been with Sir Ivor ten years. It's not a day more than seven.'

'I know,' said Sophia. 'I can't go outside the house for them. Why, look at all the cars which have followed us down here.' And indeed there had been a perfect fleet, greatly incommoded, Sophia was glad to think, by the roundabout and, to them, surely rather baffling journey via Heal's.

Lady Beech meanwhile had not been idle. It was quite uncanny what a lot of Sir Ivor's furniture, books, knick-knacks and even cooking utensils had been lent him by Lady Beech. The house was really nothing but a loan collection. She had, with great forethought, provided herself with two packets of labels, stick-on and tie-on, and by the time Sophia had finished her business, these appeared like a sort of snow-storm, scattered throughout all the rooms.

'Darling, I have just labelled a few little things of my own which dear Ivor had borrowed from me from time to time,' she said, putting a sticky one firmly on to the giant radiogram as she spoke.

'Very sensible, darling.' Sophia secured the jet tiara, an object which she had coveted from childhood. 'Good-bye, then, Larch,' she said. 'Keep the wigs, won't you, and we'll send them to the Ivor King Home of Rest. The aged singers are sure to need them, and I feel it's just what *he* would have liked.' Larch evidently thought that this idea was full of good feeling, and held open the door of the car with an approving look.

They motored back to London in silence. Sophia loved Lady Beech and would have done almost anything for her, but she knew that it would be useless to present Vocal Lodge to the Nation if Lady Beech was always to be there, sighing at whatever visitors might venture in.

'St. Anne's Hospital First Aid Post

'Darling Rudolph darling,

'Well, the Memorial Service, I mean Requiem Mass. Did you see the photograph of Luke and me with the glamorous Mgr? I thought it was quite pretty. The object behind us in silver foxes was Florence in my ex-ones. You never saw anything like the crowds outside the Oratory, and inside there were people all over the statues. When we arrived at the front pew reserved for us, who do you think was in it dressed as what? Of course Olga as a Fr. widow. You should have just seen the looks darling Lady Beech gave her. She would keep singing just like one doesn't in Papist churches, and Serge was crying out loud into a huge black-edged handkerchief, fancy at eleven in the morning, but I believe it's really because of his Blossom they say he can't stop.

'As we all came down the aisle Olga threw back her veil, and, supported by Fred, gave plucky little smiles to right and left. I forgot to say poor Fred turned up late, looking too guilty and hoping nobody would recognize him, and of course Hamish insisted on bringing him all the way up to our pew where there wasn't room, and after fearful whisperings Luke had to give up his place to the Minister. Then on the way out Olga felt faint so that she could cling to him as you will note if you see the *Tatler*.

'The whole of the stage world was there, of course, as well as all of us. Just think how old Ivor would have enjoyed it. What waste we couldn't have had it while he was alive, can't you see him choosing which wig he would wear? But you know, funny as it was in many ways I couldn't help feeling awfully sad, especially when we got outside again and saw those huge silent mournful crowds. There's no doubt the dear old creature was a sort of figurehead, and I suppose there can hardly be a soul in England who hasn't heard that—let's face it—slightly cracking voice. I thought *The Times* put it very nicely when it said that the more that golden voice was tinged with silver, the more we loved it. I hope those fiends of parachutists killed him quickly before he knew anything about it—they think so at Scotland Yard because of no cry being heard and no sign of a struggle.

'As soon as Fred had shaken off Olga she came floating up to us in her veil and began hinting that she knew more than she cared to reveal about Ivor's death. I'm afraid I was rather rude to her but really I'm getting tired of Olga in the rôle of beautiful female spy—it's becoming a bore. I've just sent her a telegram saying "Proceed John o' Groats and await further instructions. F.69." Hope she proceeds, that's all. Darling, what a heavenly idea that Floss might be a B.F.S.—so teasing for Olga if she were. Now get some leave soon and we'll proceed to her bedroom and investigate.

'Love my darling from your darling

'SOPHIA.

'PS. Did I tell you Luke is proceeding to America on a very secret mission for the F.O.? Fancy choosing that old Fascist. I must get him some Horlick's malted tablets for the 100 hours in an open boat which will almost certainly be his fate—I keep advising him to go rowing on the Serpentine to get his hand in. So here I shall be, left all alone with Florrie and her gang, isn't it terrifying for me? Should you say Heatherley and Winthrop are ones too?'

Chapter Six

SOPHIA was now designated by the newspapers as 'Wig Heiress'. The reporters pursued her from the pillars of her own front door to the Post, where Sister Wordsworth finally routed them with a hypodermic needle, in an effort to find out how she intended to dispose of her legacy. As she refused to make any statement, they invented every kind of thing. Ninety-eight Granby Gate was for sale, and Sir Luke and Lady Sophia Garfield would take up their residence at Vocal Lodge. They were only going to use it as a summer residence. They were going to pull it down and build a block of flats. (The Georgian Group, wrapped in dreams of Federal Union, stirred in its sleep on hearing this, and groaned.) They were shutting it up to avoid the rates. They were digging for victory among the Lesbian Irises. Only the truth was not told.

Luke, who really hated publicity, even when it took the form of a beautiful studio portrait of Sophia in *Vogue*, because, he said, it did him harm in the City, became very restive, and speeded up his arrangements for leaving England. Sophia spent a busy day shopping for him. Her heart smote her for not having been much nicer to him, as it did periodically, so she tried to atone in Harrod's man's shop, and he left England fully equipped as a U-boat victim. Florence saw him off at his front door and presented him with the balaclava

75

helmet, but Sophia, who accompanied him to the station, threw it out of the taxi window explaining that there was a proper machine-made one in his valise. She kissed him good-bye on the platform to the accompaniment of magnesium flares which, rather to her disappointment (because although she always looked like an elderly negress in them, she liked to see photographs of herself in the papers), were prevented by the Ministry of Information from bearing any fruit. Luke's mission was a very secret one. As a final parting present she gave him a pocket Shakespeare to read, she explained, on the desert island where his open boat would probably deposit him.

'And if you hear a loud bang in the night,' she added, as the train drew out of the station, 'don't turn over and go to sleep again.'

'Luke hates jokes and hates the war,' she said to Mary Pencill who was also on the platform, seeing off one of Trotsky's lieutenants, 'so isn't he lucky to be going to America where they have neither?'

Mary carried Sophia off to her flat when the train had gone, and they had a long and amicable talk during which they managed to avoid the subject of politics. Sophia, who was considered absolutely red by those supporters of Munich, apologists for Mussolini and lovers of Franco, Fred and Ned, was apt to feel the truest of blue Tories when in the presence of Mary whose attitude of suspicion and obstruction always annoyed her.

'Still writing on foreheads?' Mary inquired when they were settled down in front of her gas stove.

'It's all very well for you to laugh, just wait until you've got a crushed tongue and slight oozing hæmorrhage like one of the patients we had in yesterday—you'll be only too glad to have me writing on your forehead.'

'How d'you mean, yesterday? Was there an air raid —I never noticed a thing.'

'Darling, you are so dense. Practice of course. The telephone bell rings, and I answer it and it says "Southern Control speaking. Practice air raid warning Red, expect casualties." Then, some time later, a lot of unhappy-looking people are brought in out of the street in return for threepence and a cup of tea. They are labelled with a description of their injuries, then we treat them, at least the nurses do, and I write on their foreheads and take them up to the canteen for their cup of tea.'

'With their foreheads still written on?'

'Well, they get threepence, don't they? First of all, we used to practise on each other, but then Mr. Stone very sensibly pointed out what a shambles it would be if there were a real raid and real casualties were brought in and found all the personnel tied up in Thomas's splints, and so on. Think of it! So they work on this other scheme now; it seems much more professional too.'

'Well, all I can say is, if there's a raid I hope I shall be allowed to die quietly where I am.'

'Don't be defeatist, darling,' said Sophia.

The next day Sophia, looking, she thought, really

very pretty and wearing another new black hat, went off to the Horse Guards Parade where, in the presence of a large crowd, of the microphone and of cinematographers, she handed over to Fred, who accepted it on behalf of the Nation, a cardboard model of Vocal Lodge, the Shrine of Song.

Fred made a very moving speech. He spoke first, of course, about Sophia's enormously generous action, until she hardly knew where to look. He went on to say that the Shrine of Song would be a fitting memorial to one whose loss was irreparable both to Britain and to the whole world of art; the loss of a beloved citizen and venerated artist.

'And we must remember,' he went on, warming to his work, 'that Death never has the last word. When we think of the King of Song, when we pay our pious pilgrimage to Vocal Lodge, it is not of Death that we must think but of that wonderful old spirit which is still watching over us, merged with the eternal Spirit of Patriotism. The work he would have done, had he lived to do it, will now be left undone. But will it? Those who loved him—and they were not confined to this country, mind you, they mourn as we mourn in palaces and cottages the world over—those who loved him know that before he died he had intended literally to devote every breath in his body to an Ideal. He knew that if our cause is lost there will be no Song left in the world, no Music, no Art, no Joy. Lovers of music everywhere, yes and inside Germany too, will remember that the greatest singer of our time, had he not died so prematurely, was going to give his all in the struggle for Freedom. Many an Austrian, many a Czech, many a Pole, and even many a German will think of this as he plays over the well-loved gramophone records, fearful of the creeping feet behind his windows, yet determined once more to enjoy, come what may, that Golden Voice. The cause of such a man, they will think, as they listen to those immortal trills, to that historic bass, and of such an artist, must be indeed the Cause of Right. Who can tell but that the King of Song will not finally accomplish more in death than he, or any other mortal man, could ever accomplish in life.

'Oh Death! Where is thy sting? Oh Grave! Where is thy victory?'

This speech, which was extremely well received, put Fred back on his feet again with everybody except that irascible fellow who indicates daily to Britain what she should Expect.

'We learn,' he wrote the following day, 'that Vocal Lodge has been presented to the Nation to be kept as a Shrine of Song. How do we learn this news, of Empire-wide interest? Through the columns of a free Press? No! A Minister of the Crown withholds it from the public in order to announce it himself in a speech. Praise Lady Sophia Garfield, who gives. The clumsy mismanagement of the whole affair is not her fault. Examine the record of this Minister. It is far from good. We should like to see him offer his resignation forthwith and we should like to see his resignation accepted.'

However, all the other newspapers as well as Fred's colleagues thought that it was first-class stuff and that he had more or less atoned for so carelessly mislaying the King. He was extremely grateful to Sophia who had given him the opportunity for turning Sir Ivor's death to such good account. He and Ned took her out to dinner, fed her with oysters and pink champagne, and stayed up very late indeed.

Sophia, when at last she got home, was surprised and bored, as well as rather startled, to find Greta in her bedroom. She never allowed anybody to wait up for her. Greta seemed very much upset about something, her face was swollen with tears and it was several moments before she could speak.

'Oh Frau Gräfin, don't let them send me back to Germany—they will, I know it, and then in a camp they will put me and I shall die. Oh, protect me, Frau Gräfin.'

'But Greta, don't be so absurd. How can anybody send you back to Germany? We are at war with the Germans, so how could you get there? You might have to be interned here in England if you didn't pass the tribunal, you know, but I will come with you and speak to the Magistrate and I'm sure it will be quite all right. Now go to bed and don't worry any more.'

Greta seemed far from being reassured. She shivered like a nervous horse and went on moaning about the horrors of German concentration camps and how she would certainly be sent to one, unless an even worse fate was in store for her.

'You've been reading the White Paper,' said Sophia impatiently. 'And it should make you realize how very, very lucky you are to be in England.'

'Oh, please protect me,' was all Greta replied to this felicitous piece of propaganda. 'They are coming for me; it may be to-night. Oh please, Frau Gräfin, may I sleep in your bathroom to-night?'

'Certainly not. Why, you have got Mrs. Round in the very next room, and Rawlings next door to that. Much safer than being in my bathroom, and besides, I want to have a bath. Now, Greta, pull yourself together and go to bed. You have been upset by poor Sir Ivor's death, and so have we all. We must just try to forget about it, you see. Good night, Greta.'

Greta clutched Sophia's arm, and speaking very fast she said, 'If I tell you something about Sir Ivor, may I sleep in your bathroom? He is——' Her voice died away in a sort of moan, her eyes fixed upon the doorway. Sophia looked round and saw Florence standing there.

'Well, that's all now, Greta. Good night,' Sophia said. Greta slunk out past Florence, who did not give her a glance but told Sophia that she had come in search of an aspirin.

'I had to go off duty, my head ached so badly.'

'Oh, what bad luck. Would a Cachet Fèvre do as well? I've just been having such a scene with Greta; she has got it into her head that somebody is going to take her back to Germany, silly fool. I wish to goodness somebody would, I'd give anything to get rid of her.'

Florence said it was always a mistake to have foreign servants, thanked her for the Cachet Fèvre, and went upstairs. Sophia had rather been expecting that now Luke had gone perhaps Florence would be moving too, but she showed no signs of such an intention. However, the house was large, and they very rarely met, besides, she did not exactly dislike Florence; it was more that they had so little in common.

'St. Anne's Hospital First Aid Post

'My own darling Rudolph,

'Florence has joined the Post, did I tell you, and it really is rather a joke. All those terribly nice cosy ladies who have such fun with the Dowager Queen of Ruritania and whether she had Jewish blood, and whether the Crown Princess will ever have a baby and so on, are simply withered up by Flo who says she finds extraordinarily little pleasure in gossiping nowadays. They had rather fun for a time, coming clean and sharing and being guided and so on, but they never really got into it. The last straw was that Miss Edwards said she simply couldn't tell fortunes any more when Florence was there because of the atmosphere, and Miss Edwards' fortunes were the nicest thing in the Post, we all had ours done every day. Anyhow, it seems that last night the nurses went to Sister Wordsworth in a body and said that although of course Florence is very, very charming and they all liked her very, very, very much, they really couldn't stick her in the Treatment Room another moment. Sister Wordsworth is wonderful, she never turned a hair. She sent for Florence at once and asked her if, as a great favour, she would consent to take charge of the Maternity Ward, which is that little dog kennel, you know, by the Museum, with a cradle and a pair of woolly boots. As it happens, Florence is very keen on obstetrics and she was delighted. So all is honey again and the Dowager Queen of Ruritania and Miss Edwards reign supreme. Sister Wordsworth says the head A.R.P. lady in these parts is a pillar of the Brotherhood, and sent Florence with such a tremendous recommendation that she can never be sacked however much of a bore she is.

'Heatherley and Winthrop have also joined as stretcher-bearers, in fact the Brotherhood seems to be doing pretty well, just like I never thought it would. I wonder if Heth isn't a bit in love with Florence, there was a form which looked awfully like his on the half-landing when I got back late from the 400 a day or two ago. I was too terrified to look again, so I ran up to my room and locked myself in. Probably it was my imagination.

'Love my darling, when are you going to have some leave,

'SOPHIA.'

The telephone bell rang and Sophia answered it. 'Southern Control speaking. Practice RED, expect casualties.' This meant that 'casualties' would be arriving from the street. She ran up to the canteen to warn Sister Wordsworth, who was having tea.

'Thank you, Lady Sophia. Now would you go and ring up the doctor?' said Sister Wordsworth. 'If you hurry, you will catch him at his home address. He said he would like to come to the next practice we have here.'

Sophia ran downstairs again. On her way back to

the office she nearly collided with Heth and Winthrop who were carrying a stretcher.

'Casualties already!' she said, and as she was going on she noticed that the 'casualty' under the rugs on the stretcher was her own maid, Greta. For a moment she felt surprised, and then she thought that Florence must have asked Greta to do it; probably they were short of casualties. Greta was far too superior to be bribed by threepence and a cup of tea. She had a sort of bandage over her mouth, and had evidently been treated for 'crushed tongue', a very favourite accident at St. Anne's. She seemed to have something in her eye, or at any rate it was winking and rolling in a very horrible way.

Sophia, as she went to the telephone, giggled to herself. 'Typical of them,' she thought, 'to treat the wretched woman for crushed tongue when really she is half blinded by a grit in the eye. Let's hope they'll take it out and give her a cup of tea soon.' As the practice got into full swing Sophia became very busy and forgot the incident. She never saw Greta again.

Chapter Seven

THE sensation which was caused by the supposed murder of Sir Ivor King, the King of Song, at a time so extremely inconvenient to the British Government, had scarcely subsided when the old singer turned up, wig and all, in Germany. It happened on the very day that Vocal Lodge was opened to the public, a ceremony which, at the request of the A.R.P., was unadvertised, and which therefore consisted of Sophia, in a simple little black frock, dispensing cocktails to Fred, in his pin stripes, and a few other friends. The house was rather bare of furniture, owing to Lady Beech. Hardly had Fred arrived when he was called to the telephone; white to the lips he announced that he had had news which compelled him to leave for the office at once.

The German Press and Radio were jubilant. The old gentleman, it seemed, was visiting that music-loving country with the express purpose of opening there a world-wide anti-British campaign of Propaganda allied to Song. This campaign, it was considered, would have a profound effect on neutral opinion, and indeed might well bring America into the war, on one side or another. He was received like a king in Germany, the Führer sending his own personal car and bodyguard to meet him at the airport, and he celebrated his first evening in Berlin by singing 'Deutschland über Alles' on the radio in a higher and then in a lower key than it had ever been sung before.

Lord Haw-haw succeeded him at the microphone, and in his inimitable accents announced that the Lieder König was too tired to sing any more that evening but that listeners should prepare for his first full programme of Song-Propaganda in two days' time at 6.30 p.m. on the thirty-one meter band.

'You must all be most anxious to hear,' continued Lord Haw-haw, '*how* the Lieder König came to our Fatherland. (He himself will be telling you *why* he came.) Your English police, it seems, never realized that the body found on the Pagoda at Kew Gardens was, in fact, the body of a wigless pig. Had they not jumped so quickly to conclusions, had they not assumed, as, of course, they were intended to assume, that these bleeding lumps of meat did constitute the mangled body of the Lieder König, they would not, I expect, have been in such a hurry to bury them. There must be many housewives, whose husbands are at present behind the lines in France, flirting with the pretty French demoiselles, and to whom your Minister of War, Mr. Horribleisha, has not yet paid their pathetically small allowances, who would have been only too glad to dispose of these lumps of pig. For bacon is extremely scarce in England now, and is indeed never seen outside the refrigerators of the wealthy.

'Again I ask, where is the *Ark Royal*?

'Here are the stations Hamburg, Bremen and D x B, operating on the thirty-one metre band. Thank you for your attention. Our next news in English will be broadcast from Reichsender Hamburg and station Bremen at 11.15 Greenwich mean time.'

For a day or two the English newspapers assured their readers that the loyal old 'King' was really reposing in his Catholic grave, and that the Germans must be making use of gramophone records, made before the war had begun, in order to perpetrate a gigantic hoax. Alas! The 'King' only had to give his first full-length broadcast for this theory to collapse. Nobody but himself could say 'Hullo dears! Keep your hairs on' in quite that debonair tone of voice.

'I have come to Germany,' he went on, 'with the express intention of lending my services to the Fatherland, and this I do partly because I feel a debt of gratitude to this great country, this home of music where many years ago my voice was trained, but chiefly because of my love of Slavery. I have long been a member of the English Slavery Party, an underground movement of whose very existence most of you are unaware but which is daily increasing in importance. It is my intention to give bulletins of news and words of encouragement to that Party, sandwiched between full programmes of joyous song in which I hope you will all join.

> 'Land of dope you're gory
> And very much too free,
> The workers all abhor thee,
> And long for slavery.'

After bellowing out a good deal more of this kind of drivel, the 'King' told a long story about an English worker who, having been free to marry a Jewess (a thing

87

which, of course, could never happen in Germany), had been cheated out of one and sixpence by his brother-in-law.

'Now here is a word of advice to my brothers of the Slavery Party. Burn your confidential papers and anything that could incriminate you at once. Those of you who have secret stores of castor oil, handcuffs and whips waiting for the great dawn of Slavery, bury them or hide them somewhere safe. For Eden was seen entering the Home Office at 5.46 Greenwich mean time this afternoon, and presently the Black-and-Tans are to conduct a great round-up in the homes of the suspects. For the benefit of my non-British listeners, let me explain that the Black-and-Tans are Eden's dreaded police, so called because those of them that are not negroes are Mayfair play-boys, the dregs of the French Riviera. They are a brutal band of assassins, and those who fall foul of them vanish without any trace.'

Now the sinister thing about all this was that Mr. Eden really had entered the Home Office at 5.46 on the afternoon in question. How could they have known it in Berlin at 6.30? The Ministry of Information decided to suppress so disquieting a fact for the present.

By the next morning, of course, every single window of the newly constituted Shrine of Song had been broken. Lady Beech having removed all her own furniture, books, knick-knacks and kitchen utensils in three large vans, there was fortunately nothing much to damage, except the 'King's' tatty striped wallpapers. Larch and his fellow-domestics gave notice at once, and fled from the Shrine of Shame as soon as they could.

Poor Sophia felt that she had been made a fool of, and wished the beastly old fellow dead a thousand times. She communicated this sentiment to the many reporters by whom she was once more surrounded, but unfortunately, once crystallized into hard print, it did not redound entirely to her credit considering that she was the 'King's' heiress. The dignitary of the Roman Catholic Church, too, was very much displeased at having been bamboozled into allowing a Requiem Mass to be sung for the soul of a pig. Indeed Roman Catholics all over the world were aghast at the 'King's' treachery, the more so as they had always hitherto felt great pride that one so distinguished should be a co-religionist, had regarded his enormous fame as being a feather in the cap of Holy Mother Church herself, and had never forgotten the pious deeds of his late wife, the posthumous Duchess King. At last Papist feeling became so strong on the subject that the Pope, bowing before the breeze, removed the body of the posthumous Duchess from its distinguished resting-place in the Vatican gardens, and had it re-interred in the Via della Propaganda. When a German note was presented to him on the subject, he gave it as an excuse that the younger cardinals were obliged to learn bicycling on account of the petrol shortage, and were continually falling over her grave. Equally furious and disillusioned were music lovers and fans of the 'King' in the whole civilized world. His gramophone records and his effigy were burnt in market towns all over England, his wigs were burnt on Kew Green, whilst in London his songs were burnt by the public hangman.

But the person who really caught the full blast of the storm was poor Fred. He hurried round to No. 10, and did not spend anything like half-an-hour there, but only just so long as it took him to write a letter beginning 'My dear Prime Minister' and to hand over his Cabinet key. He was succeeded at the Ministry by Ned, to Ned's delight hardly veiled. The *Daily Runner* unkindly printed extracts from the 'Oh! Death! where is thy sting' speech, and crowed over Fred's resignation, but was not the least bit pleased over Ned's appointment, and suggested that it was a case of out of the frying-pan into the fire.

Fred and Sophia dined together very sadly at the Hyde Park Hotel. Ned would not risk being seen in such discredited company and kept away, and probably he was wise because, as they went into dinner, they were ambushed and subjected to withering fire by about ten press photographers. Fred could no longer afford oysters or pink champagne, so they had smoked salmon and claret instead.

He was intensely gloomy altogether. 'My career is over,' he said.

Sophia told him, 'Nonsense, think of Lord Palmerston,' but there was not much conviction in her voice.

The next day she heard that he had taken over Serge's Blossom.

'St. Anne's Hospital First Aid Post

'Oh, darling Rudolph, who ever would have thought it of the old horror?

'I must say there is one comfort to be got out of the

whole business and that is the broadcasts. Aren't they heaven? I can't keep away from them, and Sister Wordsworth has had to alter all the shifts here so that nobody shall be on the road during them. I can't ever go out in the evening because of the 10.45 one—the 6.30 I get here before I leave.

'Poor Fred sometimes sneaks round, when he can get away from his Blossom, and we listen together after dinner. His wife simply can't stand it, and I don't blame her when you think of the thousands a year it is costing them. Certainly it comes hardest on Fred, but I look a pretty good fool too what with the Requiem Mass, Shrine of Song, and so on.

'It was fortunate about Olga being a plucky Fr. widow you must say, and being photographed with Fred, otherwise how she would have crowed. I hear she was just about to proceed to John o' Groats when she guessed it was me and now she's furious so I must think up some more things to do to her. Perhaps you could think as you're in love with her—do.

'What else can I tell you? Oh yes, Greta has left, isn't it lucky? She came round here to lend a hand with a practice and hasn't been back since and apparently her luggage has all gone so I suppose she just walked out on me. I'm very pleased, I really hated having a German in the house especially as she used to be so keen on all the Nazi leaders, she gave me the creeps you know. So now Mrs. Round can talk world-politics in her own servants' hall again.

'Here everything is just the same. Florence, Heatherley and Winthrop hardly ever leave the

Maternity ward at all nowadays. I can't imagine how they squash into that tiny room. They seem to be for ever fetching food from the Canteen. I believe Brothers eat twice what ordinary people do. Anyhow they don't hurt anyone by being there, and Miss Edwards is back on the top of her form again telling the most heavenly fortunes, and isn't it funny she says she can see the same thing in all our hands, like before a railway accident, and it is SOMETHING QUEER UNDER YOUR FEET. Thank goodness not over your head because then I should have known it was para-chutists and died of fright. She thinks perhaps this place is built over a plague spot, but Mr. Stone says it must be the Main Drain and I suppose there are some pretty queer things in that all right.

'I must fly home now because the old wretch is going to sing Camp Songs (concentration camp, I suppose) at 8 for an extra treat.

'Love and xxx from
'Sophia.

'PS. There is a water pipe here which makes a noise exactly like those crickets on the islands at Cannes. Much as I hate abroad, you can hardly count Cannes and it was a heavenly summer, do you remember, when Robin lent the Clever Girl for the Sea Funeral of a Fr. solicitor from Nice and the coffin bobbed away and came up on the bathing beach at Monte Carlo. I wish it was now. Darling.'

Henceforward the doings of the Lieder König were a kind of serial story, which appeared day by day on the front pages of the newspapers, quite elbowing out the suave U-boat commanders, the joy of French poilus at seeing once more the kilt, and the alternate rumours that there would, or would not, be bacon rationing, which had so far provided such a feast of boredom at the beginning of each day. He soon became the only topic of conversation whenever two or more Englishmen met together, while the sale of wireless sets in London were reported to have gone up 50 per cent, and a hundred people of the name of King applied to change it by deed poll. His programmes were a continual treat, especially for collectors of musical curiosities, as, for instance, when he sang the first act from *La Bohème*, 'Tes petites mains sont gelées,' etc., twice through with Frau Goering, each taking alternately the male and female parts. It was after this that he suddenly gave an account of the Prime Minister walking in St. James's Park that very morning, with a list of all the birds he saw and exactly what they were doing; and although the birds, owing to the autumnal season, were behaving with absolute propriety, and therefore nobody need feel embarrassed on that score, the mere fact of such accurate knowledge having reached Berlin so quickly was disquieting to the authorities. On another occasion he sang through an entire act of *Pelléas and Mélisande*, taking all the parts himself; as a tour de force this was pronounced unique and even the *Times* musical critic was obliged to admit that the Lieder König had never, within living memory, been in better voice. A touching incident occurred some days later when Herr Schmidt, the Lieder König's music teacher, who had prophesied all those years ago in Düsseldorf that Herr King's voice would make musical history, was brought to the microphone. He was now 108 and claimed to be the oldest living music teacher. His broadcast, it is true, was not very satisfactory and sounded rather like someone blowing bubbles, but the Lieder König paid a charming tribute to the old fellow. He said that as all his success in life had been due to the careful training which he had received from Herr Schmidt, a German, he was so happy that he had the opportunity of helping the Fatherland in its time of difficulty. He and his teacher were then decorated by Herr von Ribbentrop, speaking excellent English, with the Order of the Siegfried Line, 3rd class.

Always at the end of his concerts the Lieder König announced succulent pieces of good cheer for the English Slavery Party. Soon, according to his information, vast concentration camps would spring into being all over England, to be filled with Churchill, Eden and other Marxist—here he corrected himself—Liberals, Jews and plutocrats.

Soon the benevolent rule of National Socialism would stretch across the seas to every corner of the British and French Empires, harnessing all their citizens to the tyrant's yoke, and removing the last vestiges of personal freedom. Soon all nations of the world would be savouring the inestimable advantages of Slavery.

'Here are the Reichsender Bremen, stations Hamburg and D x B operating on the thirty-one metre band. This is the end of the Lieder König's talk in English.'

Chapter Eight

SOPHIA was dressing to go out to dinner with Fred, Ned and Lady Beech. She took a good deal of trouble always with her appearance, but especially when she was going to be seen in the company of Lady Beech, whose clothes were the most exquisite in London and whom it was not possible in that respect to outshine. Sophia had not attempted to replace Greta and was beginning to realize what an excellent maid that boring German had been; on this occasion she could not find anything she wanted, nor was Elsie, the housemaid, very much help to her.

Sophia was a very punctual character, with the result that she often found herself waiting for people, and indeed must have spent several weeks of her life, in all, waiting for Rudolph. On this occasion Fred and she arrived simultaneously and first, in spite of the many setbacks in her bedroom. He ordered her a drink and muttered in her ear that Ned was behaving as if he had been in the Cabinet all his life. It seemed anyhow that he felt himself firmly enough in the saddle after three Cabinet meetings to be able once more to consort with those victims of circumstances, Fred and Sophia. But of course Fred in the uniform pertaining to his Blossom was hardly at all reminiscent of Fred in the pin-stripe trousers of his disgrace; he looked already brown and healthy and seemed to have grown quite an inch.

Lady Beech appeared next, wonderful in sage green and black with ostrich feathers and a huge emerald laurel leaf. Sophia felt at once extremely dowdy.

'You are lucky,' she said, 'the way you always have such heavenly things. I do wish I were you.'

'Child!' said Lady Beech, deprecatingly.

Very late the Minister himself galloped up to them complaining loudly that he had been kept at No. 10. As his own house happened to be No. 10 Rufford Gate, there was a pleasing ambiguity about this excuse. They went in to dinner.

Fred and Ned were very partial to Lady Beech. She was the only link they had with culture, and Fred and Ned were by no means so insensible to things of the mind as they appeared to be. At school and at Oxford they had been clever boys with literary gifts and a passion for the humanities; it was only their too early excursion into politics which had reduced their intellectual capacity once more to that of the private school. The poor fellows still felt within them a vague yearning towards a higher plane of life, and loved to hear Lady Beech discourse, in polished accents now sadly unfamiliar, of Oscar, Aubrey, Jimmy, Algernon, Henry, Max, Willie, Osbert and the rest. They could talk to her, too, of those of their contemporaries whose lives had taken a more intellectual turn than their own, for Lady Beech is as much beloved by the present as she was by a past generation of artists and writers. Another thing which endeared her to them was the fact that she, unlike anybody else, called them Sir Frederick and Lord Edward and, instead of telling them her opinion of The Situation, flatteringly deferred to theirs. It made them feel positively grown up. She liked them, too; they were such pretty, polite young men, and she particularly liked oysters and pink champagne. When, on this occasion, they suggested that a little white wine would be suitable because of the income tax, and the fact that poor Fred had so little income left to tax, she sighed very dreadfully indeed and they good naturedly reverted to pre-war rations for that evening. The dinner having been ordered to her entire satisfaction, Lady Beech turned to Ned with her usual opening gambit of, 'Tell me, Lord Edward.' This was really rather horrid of her as, hitherto, it had always been, 'Tell me, Sir Frederick.'

'Tell me what you think will happen?'

Ned opened his napkin and said cheerfully, 'Oh gracious, I don't know. Nothing much, I don't expect.'

'Ah! You mean there will be no allied offensive for the moment?'

'Hullo, there's Bob! Well, now, Lady Beech, you won't quote me, will you? I never said that, you know. But between ourselves, quite between, well I rather expect we shall all go bumbling along as we are doing until we have won the war—or lost it, of course.'

'Should you say there was quite a good possibility of that?'

'Of what?'

'Of our losing the war?'

'Oh quite a good chance, oh Lord yes. Mind you, of course, we're bound to win really, in the end, we always do. All I say is it may be a long business, the way we're setting about it. Well, Fred, so how's the balloon these days, eh?'

'Up and down, you know. It's rather like playing a salmon, getting her down. I enjoy it. Frankly I enjoy it more than—oh well, it's a healthy outdoor life.'

'Should you say,' asked Lady Beech, 'that the balloons are of much use?'

'I'm told none whatever,' said Ned in his loud jolly voice.

'Ah!' she looked searchingly at Fred who was quite nettled.

'That's entirely a matter of opinion,' he said crossly. 'I should think myself they are a jolly sight more use than—oh well. Anyway, it's a healthy outdoor life for the lads who do it, which is more than you can say for —well, some other kinds of lives.'

'Do you think you can keep off the parachutists?' said Sophia. 'They are the only thing I mind. Give me bombs, gas, anything you like. It's the idea of those sinister grey-clad figures, with no backs to their heads, slowly floating past one's bedroom window like snowflakes that gives me the creeps.'

'They would not be grey-clad,' Ned assured her. 'If they come at all, which is very unlikely (not that the balloons would stop them) they will be dressed as Guards' officers.'

'Lean out of your window and break their legs with a poker as they go by,' suggested Fred.

Lady Beech now broke the ice by saying, 'I was listening to my poor old brother-in-law on the wireless before I came out.'

Everybody had, of course, been dying to begin on this topic but none of the others had liked to, Sophia because of poor Fred, poor Fred because he knew that Lady Beech was the 'King's' sister-in-law, and Ned because, although the least sensitive person in the world, he did feel it was perhaps hardly for him to do so, having made such good capital out of Sir Ivor's defection.

Lady Beech went on, 'He was giving a concert of Mozart, and I must tell you that it was perfectly exquisite. Schumann herself could not have given such an ideal rendering of *Voi che sapete*—I never heard such notes, never.'

'Yes, the old beast can sing,' Fred muttered gloomily.

'I wonder what he feels like,' said Sophia. 'I mean, when he thinks of all of us he must be rather sad. He did so love jokes, too, and I don't suppose he gets many of them, or at any rate people to share them with.'

'It is so strange,' said Lady Beech, 'oh, it is so strange! As you know, I was very intimate indeed with him, and I should have said that he had a particularly strong love of his country, and of his own people. He was so attached to you, darling, and to all his friends—I think I may add, to me.' She sighed. The disposition of Vocal Lodge, although it had proved to be premature, still rankled a little with her. 'Well, there it is. I shall never understand it, never, it seems to me that it can't be true, and yet—— Tell me, Lord Edward, is it possible that he is doing this with some motive that we know nothing about?'

'I couldn't say. I suppose the old buffer gets well paid, what?'

'Oh, you don't know Ivor if you think that would have anything to do with it. He never cared the least bit for money. He had far too much of it for his needs. Why should he want more?'

'I put it down to a morbid love of publicity,' said Fred. He could not speak without bitterness of the wrecker of his career.

'But he would have had publicity under your scheme, Sir Frederick, and with it love and praise instead of hatred and contempt.'

'Depends which way you look at it. I expect he gets love and praise in Germany all right.'

'I can't believe that that is much comfort to him. He never cared for Germany as far as I knew; he certainly never sang there. I should have said he cared for nothing, these last years, but his garden. He was even neglecting his voice in order to be able to work longer hours among his cabbages. I reproached him for it.'

'Perhaps they promised him a whole mass of Lesbian Irises.'

'Perhaps they caught him and tortured him until he said he would sing for them.'

'Ah, now that I think is very probably the explanation,' said Lady Beech with mournful satisfaction. 'And curiously enough, just the one that had occurred to me. Terrible, terrible. What should you say they do to him, Lord Edward?'

'Oh, really, I don't know much about these things. Thumbscrew, I suppose, then there was the rack, the boot and the *peine forte et dur*, but I always think a night-light under the sole of the foot would be as good as anything.'

'Do stop,' said Sophia, putting her fingers in her ears. She could never bear to hear of tortures.

'Actually I wonder if he would do it with such gusto if he had the thumbscrew hanging over him, so to speak. I mean he does get the stuff off his chest as if he really enjoyed it—eh?'

'You forget,' said Lady Beech, 'that Ivor was nothing if not an artist. Once he began to sing he would be certain to do it well, whatever the circumstances. That he could not help.'

'Oh, poor old gentleman,' said Sophia, 'it would really have been better for him to have died on Kew Pagoda all along.'

'Very, very much better,' said Lady Beech. 'Now, tell me, Lord Edward (I am changing the subject to one hardly less painful) supposing, I say *supposing* anybody had a very small sum of money to invest, what should you yourself advise doing with it? I don't mean speaking as a Member of the Cabinet; I just want your honest advice.'

'Personally,' said Ned, brightening up, 'I should put it on a horse. I mean, a sum like that, the sort of sum you describe, is hardly worth saving, is it? Why not go a glorious bust on Sullivan in the 3.30 to-morrow?'

'You wouldn't say that if you knew how unlucky I am, would he, child?' she said to Sophia; 'but what I really wanted to know about is these defence loans, to buy or not to buy? I thought you could advise me.'

Ned gave a guilty jump and said the defence loans

were just the very thing for her. 'I bought a certificate for my little nipper to-day,' he said, 'but the little blighter wanted it in hard cash. Couldn't blame the kid either—I mean, of course, at that age. In fifteen years he'll be glad—if he's not dead. Well,' he looked importantly at his watch, 'I must be getting back to No. 10.'

'Child,' said Lady Beech, 'have you got Rawlings with you? No? Then perhaps Lord Edward will escort me to a bus.'

Fred and Sophia decided to make a night of it. They went to several very gay restaurants and then to a night club. Here, many hours after they had left the Carlton, Fred talked about his Ideals. It seemed that, at night, as he watched his Blossom careering about among the stars, Ideals had come to Fred, and he had resolved, should he ever again achieve Cabinet rank, that he would be guided by them.

'I used to go on, you know, from day to day, doing things just as they came without any purpose in my life. But now it will be different.'

Sophia had heard this kind of talk before; it sounded horribly as though the Brotherhood was claiming another victim. Apparently however, this time it was Federal Union, and Fred expounded its theories to her at great length.

'So what d'you think of it?' he said when he had finished.

'Well, darling, I didn't quite take it in. I feel rather deliciously muzzy to tell you the truth, you know the

102

feeling, like that heavenly anæsthetic they give you nowadays.'

'Oh.' Fred was disappointed.

'Tell me again, darling, and I'll listen more carefully.'

He told her.

'Well, if it means the whole world is going to be ruled by the English, I'm all for it."

'Oh no, it's not like that at all; I must have explained it badly.'

He began again, taking enormous trouble.

Presently someone Sophia knew came up to their table. Sophia was feeling extremely vague. She introduced Fred as Sir Frederick Union. After this he took her home.

Chapter Nine

THE Lieder König had just finished one of his Pets'
Programmes. These were a terrible thorn in the side of
the authorities, who considered that all the other pieces
in his repertoire were exceedingly harmless, although
the news which was thrown in at the end always included some item proving that the German Secret
Service arrangements for transmitting facts to Berlin
had ours beat by about twelve hours, and this certainly
did tease the M.I. rather. But the Pets' Programmes
were a definite menace. Playing upon the well-known
English love of animals the wily Hun provided this
enormous treat for the pets of the United Kingdom.

'Bring your Bow-wow, your Puss-puss, your Dickie-
bird, your Moo-cow, your Gee-gee, your Mousie and
your three little fishes to the radio. Or, take the radio
out to the stables if your pets cannot be brought indoors.
For those raising hens on the battery system these
concerts should prove profitable indeed—few hens can
resist laying an egg after hearing the Lieder König.
The real object of these programmes is not, however, a
mercenary one, the object is to bring joy to the hearts
of dumb creatures, too many of whom spend a joyless
life without song. There is no need for your pets to
belong to this category any more; bring them all to the
radio and see what pleasure you will give them. The
Lieder König himself, who can sing so high that bats

can hear him, and so low that buffaloes can, is here expressly to minister to your dumb ones, and bring them strength through joy.'

The old gentleman then came to the radio and gave first a little talk about the muddle of animal A.R.P. in London. Few dogs and no cats, he said, carried gas masks, and gas-proof cages for birds and mice were the exception rather than the rule. The animal first-aid posts were scandalously few and ill equipped. The evacuation scheme had not been a success, and many mothers of dogs had fetched their little ones home rather than unselfishly bear the parting for their sakes. 'I dedicate this concert to the animal evacuees in strange homes,' he said, 'may they think of England and stay away from London until this stupid war is over. Here in Germany you hardly ever see a pet; all the dogs are at the West Wall, and the rest are nobly playing their part, somewhere.' He then delivered a series of shrieks and groans which certainly did have an uncanny effect upon any animals who happened to listen in. Dogs and cats joined in the choruses, horses danced upon their hind legs, and dickie birds went nearly mad with joy. Mice crept out of their holes to listen, while in the country the radio on these occasions proved such a magnet to frogs and snails and slugs that many people thankfully used it as a trap for small garden pests. The authorities at the Zoo had gramophone records made to cheer up their charges during the black-out, and Ming, the panda, would soon eat no food until one of them was played to her.

The results of all this can readily be imagined. On the

day after one of these concerts Members of Parliament would be inundated by a perfect flood of letters from sentimental constituents demanding instant cessation of hostilities against our fellow animal-lovers, the Germans. In fact, the Pets' Programme did more for the enemy cause over here than all the broadcasts by Lord Haw-haw, all the ravings of the Slavery Party's organ, *The New Bondsman*, and all the mutterings of Bloomsbury's yellow front put together.

'If the pets all over the world,' concluded the Lieder König, 'were to rise up as one pet and demand peace, peace we should have.'

'Here are the Reichsender Bremen, stations Hamburg and D x B operating on the 31 metre band. The Lieder König wishes to thank all pets for listening. The next Pets' Concert will be on Tuesday next at 9.45.'

Sophia and Fred, who had dined with her, had been listening, for the benefit of those returned evacuees, Milly and Abbie. Sophia had sent for Milly, against her better judgment, because she did not get along without her very well, and also for protection from the parachutists. She was a French bulldog, as clever as she was beautiful, and Abbie was her daughter. Abbie's blood was mixed, Milly having thrown herself away upon a marmalade Don Juan, one spring morning in Westminster Abbey, but she was very sweet and the apple of Fred's eye. When the Pets' Programme was over, they took their leave, Sophia going a little way up the Square with them in order to give Milly a run after her emotional experience. When they got back, Milly galloped upstairs and burrowed her way under Sophia's quilt until she came to where the hot-water bottle was, when she flopped at once into a snoring sleep.

Sophia followed more slowly. She had a pain which had not been improved by her excursion into the cold. When she reached her bathroom she looked for the Cachets Fèvre, but presently remembered that she had given the box to Florence, and went up the next flight of stairs to Florence's bedroom. She knocked on the door without much expecting any reply: when there was none, she went in.

She had not seen the room since Florence had occupied it, and was quite shocked to see how much it had been subdued. Pretty and frilly as it was, like any room done up by Sophia, Florence had done something intangible to it by her mere presence, and it was looking frightful. The dressing-table, exquisite with muslin, lace, roses and blue bows, like a ball dress in a dream, and which was designed to carry an array of gold-backed brushes, bottles, pots of cream and flagons of scent, was bare except for one small black brush and a comb which must have originally been meant for a horse's mane. The Aubusson carpet had its pattern of lutes and arrows, with more roses and blue bows, completely obscured by two cheap-looking suitcases. A pair of stays and a gas-mask case had been thrown across the alluring bed cover, puckered with pink velvet and blue chiffon. Sophia, who herself wore a ribbon suspender-belt, looked in horrified fascination at the stays. 'No wonder Florence is such a queer shape,' she thought, picking them up, 'she will never be a glamour girl in stays like that, and how does she get into them?' She held them against her own body but could not make out which bit went where; they were like medieval armour. As she put them back on the bed she saw that the gas-mask carrier contained a Leica camera instead of a gas mask, and she thought it was simply horrible of Florence never to have taken a photograph of Milly with it. The pigeon, in its cage, was dumped on a beautiful satinwood table, signed by Sheraton; considering how much Florence was supposed to love it, she might have provided it with a larger cage. The poor thing was shuffling up and down miserably. Sophia stroked its feathers with one finger through the wire netting, and remembered a beautiful Chippendale bird-cage for sale in the Brompton Road. She might give it to Florence for Christmas, but Florence seemed so very indifferent to pretty objects. Perhaps, she thought, the bird wants to go out. She opened the cage, took it in her hands, stroked it for a while, and put it out of the window, just too late, evidently, for it made a mess on her skirt.

When she had shut the window and wiped her skirt, Sophia felt an impulse to tidy up; it was really too annoying of Elsie, the housemaid, to leave the room in such a mess. She put away the stays and gasmask case, and then took hold of a hatbox, intending to take it upstairs to the boxroom, but although, as she did so, the top opened, revealing that it was quite empty inside, it was so heavy that she could hardly lift it, so she gave up the idea. Really, her pain was quite bad and she must find the cachets. She opened a few drawers, but they were all full of papers. Then she remembered that there were some shelves in the built-in cupboard so she opened that.

In the part of the cupboard which was meant for dresses stood Heatherley Egg.

Sophia's scream sounded like a train going through a tunnel. Then she became very angry indeed.

'Stupid,' she said, 'to frighten me like that. Anyway, what's the point of waiting in Florence's cupboard—she's on duty, doesn't come off till six.'

Heatherley slid out into the room and gripped her arm. 'Listen,' he said, 'we have got to get this straight.'

'Oh, don't let's bother,' said Sophia, who had lost interest now that she had recovered from her fright. 'God knows I'm not a prude, and Florence's private life has nothing to do with me. Live in her cupboard if you like to; I don't care.'

'See here, Sophia, you can't get away with that. Now, sit down; we have to talk this over.'

'You haven't seen some Cachets Fèvre anywhere, have you? I lent her a box and, of course, she didn't bring them back; people never do, do they? It doesn't matter to speak of, I must go to bed. Well, good night, Heatherley. What about breakfast? Do you like it in your own cupboard, or downstairs?'

She went towards the door.

'Oh, no you don't!' said Heatherley, in quite a menacing sort of voice, very different from his usual transatlantic whine. 'You can't fool me that way, Sophia. Very clever, and I should have been quite taken in, but I happened to watch you through the keyhole. Those bags have false bottoms, haven't they, the gas-mask contains a camera, doesn't it, and there are code signals sewn into the stuffing of those stays. Eh?'

'Are there, how simply fascinating! Is that why they are so bumpy? Do go on!'

'Quite an actress, aren't you, and I might easily have believed you if you hadn't sent off the pigeon with a phoney message.'

'The dear thing asked to go out.'

'Yes, knowing how stupid you are, Sophia, I might have believed that everything had passed over your head, but you can't laugh off that pigeon. So come clean now; you've known the whole works since Greta disappeared, haven't you?'

'What works? Darling Heth, do tell me; it does sound such heaven.'

'As you know so much already, I guess I better had, too, tell you everything. Florence, of course, as you are no doubt aware, is a secret agent, working under a pseudonym, and with a false American passport. Her real name is Edda Eiweiss and she is the head of the German espionage in this country.'

'You don't say so! Good for Florence,' said Sophia. 'I never thought she would have had the brains.'

'Gee, Florence is probably the cleverest, most astute and most daring secret agent alive to-day.'

'Do go on. What are you? Florence's bottle-washer?'

'Why no, not at all. I am engaged in counter-espionage on behalf of the Allied Governments, but Florence, of course, believes that I am one of her gang. Now, what I want to know is, are you employed by anybody, or are you on your own?'

'But neither,' said Sophia, opening her eyes very wide.

'Sophia, I want an answer to my question, please. I have laid my cards on the table; let's have a look at yours.'

'Oh, on my own, of course,' said Sophia. As Heatherley seemed to be crediting her with these Machiavellian tactics it would be a pity to undeceive him.

'I thought so. Now, Sophia, I need your help. A woman's wits are just what I lack, so listen carefully to me. I have found out a great deal, but not all, about the German system of espionage. By November 10th, I shall have all the facts that will enable the Government to round up the entire corps of spies at present operating in this country. On that day we can catch the gang, Florence and her associates, but not before. Will you come in on this with me, Sophia?' He clutched her shoulders and stared with his light blue eyes into her face. 'Before you answer, let me tell you that it is difficult and dangerous work. You risk death, and worse, if you undertake it, but the reward, to a patriotic soul, is great.'

'Rather, of course I will.' Sophia was delighted. She, and not Olga, was now up to the neck in a real-life spy story.

'Understand, you must take all your orders from me. One false step might render useless my work of months.'

'Yes, yes.'

'And not act on your own initiative at all?'

'No, no.'

'Sophia, you are a brave woman and a great little patriot. Shake.' They shook.

'Can I ask you a question?'

'Go right ahead.'

'Well, what happened to Greta in the end?'

'What did she say to you?' asked Heatherley, with a searching look.

'I don't understand.'

'What did she say when you saw her in the Post on that stretcher?'

'Well, but she couldn't speak. She had a sort of bandage on her tongue, you see.'

'Sophia,' Heatherley's voice again took on that horrid rasping tone, 'you promised to be perfectly frank with me. Come clean now, what was she doing with her eyes?'

'Oh, her eyes. Yes, she must have had a great grit in one of them, I should imagine. She was blinking like mad; I had quite forgotten.'

'She was winking out a message to you in Morse Code. What was that message, Sophia? No double crossing——'

'My dear Heatherley, however should I know?'

'You don't know Morse Code?'

Sophia saw that she might just as well have admitted to an Ambassador of the old school that she knew no French. She decided that as she did long to be a counter-spy with Heatherley and that as she could quite quickly learn the Morse Code (she knew that stupid looking Girl Guides managed to do so) there would be no harm in practising a slight deception.

'Semaphore perfect,' she said airily. 'But I must confess my Morse needs brushing up. And anyhow, if you remember, I was running to the telephone when I passed you in that dark passage and had no time at all to see what Greta was winking about. She was such a bore, anyway, I never could stick her. So what happened to her after that?'

Heatherley pursed his lips. 'I'm afraid, my dear Sophia, that it was not very pleasant,' he said. 'You must remember that my job is counter-espionage, that I have to suppress my own personal feelings rigidly, and that very very often I am obliged to do things which are obnoxious to me.'

'Like in Somerset Maugham's books?'

'Just like—I am glad you appreciate my point. Well, it seems that Florence wasn't feeling any too sure about Greta, who was, of course, one of her corps, and was particularly anxious that Greta should not come up before the Alien's tribunal as she would probably have made mistakes and given them all away, Florence and the rest of them. Also her papers were not foolproof. So, at Florence's bidding, of course, Winthrop and I carried her on the stretcher, just as you saw her, gagged and bound, and put her into the main drain which flows, as you may not know, under the First Aid Post.'

Sophia screamed again. Heatherley went on, 'Yes, my dear Sophia, counter-espionage is a dangerous, disagreeable profession. I should like you to remember this and be most careful, always, how you act. It is absolutely necessary for you to trust me and do exactly what I say on every occasion. We are in this together now, remember, you and I.'

Sophia did not so much care about being in anything

with Heatherley, and hoped that all this would not lead
to being in bed with him; she seemed to remember that
such things were part of the ordinary day's work of
beautiful female spies. On the other hand, she felt that
she would, if necessary, endure even worse than death
in order to be mixed up in this thrilling real life spy
drama. The horrible end of poor Greta served to show
that here was the genuine article. Fancy. The main
drain. Sophia shuddered. No wonder Miss Edwards
saw something queer going on under her feet.

'Now, Sophia, I hope you realize,' Heatherley said,
'that whatever happens you are not to tell a living soul
about all this. You and I are watched day and night by
unseen eyes. These are evil things that we are fighting—
yes, evil, and very clever. The telephone, to this house
and to the Post, is tapped by Florence's men; our letters
are read and our movements followed. We may have got
away with this conversation simply by daring to hold it
here, in the heart of the enemy country; on the other
hand, we may not. As you leave this room, masked men
may seize upon us and carry us, on stretchers, to the
fate which befel you know who. Of course, if you were
to go to anybody in authority with this tale, the gang
would know it, and would disperse like a mist before the
sun—at the best my work of months would be destroyed,
at the worst you and I would suffer the supreme penalty.
I may tell you that the War Office and Scotland Yard
are watching over us in their own way, and I have
secret means of communicating with them. By the 10th
November, as I told you before, I shall have all the
evidence I need, and then the whole lot can be rounded

up. Meanwhile, you and I, Sophia, must be a team. Now you should go back to your room; this conversation has already lasted too long. I shan't be able to speak to you like this again until all is over, so REMEMBER.'

Heatherley squeezed back into his cupboard, and Sophia, highly elated and with her pain quite forgotten, skipped off and slid down the banisters to her own landing. They had evidently got away with that conversation all right, as no masked men pounced out on her and she was soon in bed, kicking Milly off the warm patch which she wanted for her own feet.

Chapter Ten

WHEN Sophia awoke the next day, she had the same feeling with which, as a child, she had greeted Christmas morning, or the day of the Pantomime. A feeling of happy anticipation. At first, and this also was like when she was little, she could not even remember what it was all about; she simply knew that something particularly lively was going to happen.

Elsie, the housemaid, called her and put a breakfast tray in front of her on which there were coffee, toast and butter, and a nice brown boiled egg, besides a heap of letters and *The Times*. Sophia had woken up enough to remember that she was now a glamorous female spy; she put on a swansdown jacket, sat up properly, and admonished Milly for refusing to go downstairs.

'Drag her,' she said to Elsie. Elsie dragged, and they left the room with a slow, shuffling movement, accompanied by the bedside rug.

The letters looked dull; Sophia began on her egg, and was attacking it with vigour when she saw that something was written on it in pencil. Not hard-boiled, she hoped. Not at all. The writing was extremely faint, but she could make out the word AGONY followed by 22.

Sophia was now in agony, for this must be, of course, a code. She knew that spies and counter-spies had the most peculiar ways of communicating with each other, winking in Morse and so on; writing on eggs would be everyday work for them. She abandoned the delicious egg, done so nicely to a turn, and rolled her eyes round the pink ceiling with blue clouds of her bedroom while she tried the word AGONY backwards and forwards and upside down. She made anagrams of the letters. She looked at the egg in her looking-glass bed-post, but all in vain. She would have to get hold of the Chief at once, but how was she to do that? Impossible to send Elsie upstairs with instructions to see if Mr. Egg was still in Miss Turnbull's cupboard, if so, Lady Sophia's compliments and would he step downstairs. In any case he was unlikely to have remained in the cupboard all night, and Florence's bed, a narrow single one, would not harbour any but impassioned lovers with the smallest degree of comfort. This, she somehow felt, Florence and Heatherley were not.

Elsie now returned with Milly, who once more dived under the eiderdown, and, with a piercing snore, resumed her slumbers.

'Did she do anything?'

'Yes, m'lady.'

'Good girl. Would you be very kind,' said Sophia, 'and go and ask Miss Turnbull if she would give me Mr. Egg's telephone number. Say I'm short of a man for to-night.'

Florence, who had only come off duty at six, was displeased at being woken up. She was understood by Elsie to say that Mr. Egg had gone to Lympne for the day, and had her ladyship remembered that there was to be a Brotherhood meeting at 98 that evening.

Sophia saw that she had been rather dense. Of course

she might have realized that if Heth had been available to see her there would have been no need for him to write on her egg. Then she saw light.

'He, Egg, is in agony, because he is unable 2 see me before 2 night.' Sophia turned to her breakfast with a happy appreciation both of its quality and of her own brilliance.

She picked up *The Times* and read about the Pets' Programme. It seemed to have fallen very flat with the musical critic. 'Not with Milly though.' Then, without looking at the war news, which she guessed would be dull, she turned to the front page and read, as she always did, the agony column. She usually found one or two advertisements that made her feel happy, and to-day there was a particularly enjoyable one. 'Poor old gentleman suffering from malignant disease would like to correspond with pretty young lady. Box 22 *The Times*.'

When Sophia had finished laughing she became quite wistful. She always called Sir Ivor the poor old gentleman, and he called her the pretty young lady. If only he were not being a dreadful old traitor in Berlin, she would have cut the advertisement out and sent it to him. 'I never should have expected to miss him as much as I do, but the fact is there are certain jokes which I can only share with him. Funny thing too,' she thought, 'suffering from malignant disease, just what he is. National Socialism.' She cut out the advertisement and put it in her jewel case, deciding that if she ever had the opportunity to do so, through neutrals, she would send it to Sir Ivor in the hopes of making him feel small. Her blood boiled as she thought again of his treachery and of the programme of Camp songs, which was exactly similar to one he had given before the Chief Scout some months previously, and which had included that prime and perennial favourite:

'There was a bee i ee i ee,
Sat on a wall y all y all y all y all,
It gave a buzz y wuz y wuz y wuz y wuz,
And that was all y all y all y all y all.'

Sir Ivor and Dr. Goebbels between them had altered the words of this classic to:

'The British E i ee i ee,
Sat on a wall y all y all y all y all,
Like Humpty Dumpt y ump ty ump ty ump ty ump,
It had a fall y all y all y all y all.'

So queer it seemed, and so horrible, that somebody who had had the best that England can give should turn against her like that. Sir Ivor had received recognition of every kind, both public and private, from all parts of the British Empire, of his great gifts. Had he been one of those geniuses who wither in attics, it would have been much more understandable. Sophia got out of bed, and while her bath was running in she did a few exercises in order to get fit for the dangers and exactions of counter-espionage.

On the way to St. Anne's, Sophia bought a Manual of Morse Code which she fully intended to learn that day. When she arrived however she found, greatly to her disgust, that, as it was Thursday, there was a great heap of clean washing to be counted.

She supposed that she must have a brain rather like that of a mother bird who, so the naturalists tell us, cannot count beyond three; counting the washing was her greatest trial. There would be between twenty and thirty overalls to be checked and put away in the nurses' pigeonholes in the 'dressing-room' which was a sacking partition labelled, rather crudely, Female. Now Sophia, with an effort of concentration, could stagger up to twelve or thirteen; having got so far the telephone bell would ring, somebody would come and ask her a question, or her own mind would stray in some new direc- tion. Then she would have to begin all over again.

It generally took her about an hour before she could make the numbers tally twice, and even then it was far from certain that they were correct. On this occasion she made them alternately twenty-five and twenty-eight, so she assumed the more optimistic estimate to be the right one, and stowed them away in their pigeon-holes. She was longing to tell Sister Wordsworth about Greta and the main drain, but of course that would never do. She did ask Mr. Stone whether the drain really flowed underneath the First Aid Post and could she see it, to which he replied that it did, and that she could, but in his opinion she would not enjoy such an experience.

'Rats,' he said. Sophia thought of Greta and shud- dered. 'As a matter of fact,' he went on, 'some fellows are going down there this evening to have a look round. I expect you could go with them if you like.'

Sophia asked what time, and when she was told at

half-past ten, she declined the offer. It would require a bigger bribe than the main drain to get her back to St. Anne's when her work there was finished.

She spent the rest of the day learning Morse Code, partly because she wished to be a well equipped counter-spy and partly (and this spurred her to enormous industry) so that she could wink at Olga in it the next time they met. There was a photograph of Olga in that week's *Tatler* wearing a black velvet crinoline with a pearl cross, and toying with a guitar, beneath which was written the words, 'This Society beauty does not require a uniform for her important war work.'

Sophia, thinking of this, redoubled her efforts of dot and dash. But she found it far from easy, even more difficult than counting overalls, though the reward of course was greater. She sat, winking madly into her hand looking- glass, until she was off duty, by which time she knew the letters A, B and C perfectly, and E and F when she thought very hard. The opportunity for showing off her new accomplishment came that evening. She had gone on duty at the Post earlier than usual, as Sister Wordsworth wanted to go out; leaving it correspondingly early, she was on her way home when she remembered that her house would be full of Brothers. So she looked in at the Ritz. Here the first person she saw was Rudolph, and sitting beside him was a heaving mass of sables which could only conceal the beautiful Slavonic person of La Gogothska herself, in the uniform, so to speak, of her important war-work.

'Hullo, my darling,' said Rudolph, fetching a chair for her. 'You're off very early. I'm dining with you to-night, though you may not know it. Elsie said I could, and she's telling your cook.'

'Good,' said Sophia, without listening much. Her eyes were fixed upon Olga and she was working away with concentration.

'What are you making those faces at me for?' said Olga crossly.

'Dear me,' said Sophia, 'how disappointing. It was just a bet I had with Fred. I betted him sixpence that you were in the secret service, he was so positive you couldn't be, and I said I could prove it. Well, I have proved it, and I have lost sixpence, that's all.'

'What do you mean?'

'Well, darling, I was just telling you, in Morse Code, to proceed to the ladies' cloakroom, and are you proceeding? No. Have you made any excuse for not doing so? No. Therefore, as you evidently don't know Morse Code which is a sine qua non for any secret agent, you can't be that beautiful female spy we all hoped you were.' Actually, of course, Sophia had only been winking out, and with great trouble at that, A, B and C.

Olga said, 'Nonsense. Morse Code is never used in this war; it's completely out of date. Why, what would be the use of it?' and she gave a theatrically scornful droop of the eyelids.

'Well, as a matter of fact, dear, it would be a very great deal of use indeed under certain circumstances. Supposing one happened to be gagged, for an example, it would be possible to wink out messages to the bystanders which, if they understood Morse, would save one's life '

'Gagged,' said Olga, shrugging her shoulders. 'Gagged indeed. Bystanders! Darling, you have been reading Valentine Williams, I suppose. Let me tell you that in real life the secret service is very different from what the outside public, like you, imagine it to be. Gagged! No, really, I must tell the Chief that.'

'Do,' said Sophia. 'He'll roar, I should think. Naturally, I don't know much about these things. Well, then, what shall I do with the sixpence?'

'I'll tell you when the war is over. Are you working very hard in your little First Aid Post? Poor Olga is overwhelmed with work. Figure to yourselves, last night I was up till six—even the Chief with his iron constitution was half dead. I had to keep on making cups of black coffee for him, and even so he fell asleep twice. Of course, the responsibility is very wearing, especially for the Chief—if things went wrong, it doesn't bear thinking of, what would happen. My knowledge of Russian, however, is standing us in good stead.'

Olga had learnt Russian when she was courting Serge, to but little avail so far as he was concerned, as he did not know a word of it. However, as she had taken the name of Olga, broken her English accent, and in other ways identified herself with the great country of Serge's forbears, she rather liked to be able to sing an occasional folk-song from the Steppes in its original tongue. She felt that it put the finishing touches to her part of temperamental Slav.

'I wonder they don't send you to Russia. I hear they find it very difficult to get reliable information.'

'Darling, it would be certain death.'

'Oh, yes, I forgot. You would be handed over to the grandchildren of Serge's grandfather's peasantry, wouldn't you? Very unpleasant. But couldn't you go disguised as a member of the proletariat in no silk stockings and drab clothes? I could give you lots of hints. You share a room with about seven other people and their bulldogs if they have any, and you have no pleasures of any kind. I really think, speaking Russian as you do, that you ought to volunteer.'

'Far, far too dangerous. The Chief would never let me. I may of course have to go abroad later—to Egypt, Turkestan or Wazuristan perhaps, but Russia is entirely out of the question. '

'I call it very cowardly of you,' said Sophia, 'your country should come first. Well, good-bye, I must be going,' and she winked out rather innacurately A, B and C. 'I'm sure the Chief would raise your screw if you knew a bit of Morse,' she said, and got up to go, followed by Rudolph who quite shamelessly left Olga to pay for the drinks.

'Think how rich she must be with all that spying,' he said happily, and kissed Sophia a great deal in the taxi. 'Darling, heavenly to see you. I've got a fortnight's leave.'

'What were you doing with Baby Bagg?'

'Just met her in the Ritz.'

'After you had telephoned to tell her to go there, I suppose.'

'Well, darling, in point of fact, I do feel rather intrigued about Olga's job. I have a sort of feeling that there may be more in that little woman than meets the eye, and I must say she's remarkably secretive. Now if you were a beautiful female spy, my own precious poppet, we should all know all about it in two days. For one thing of course, you would never be able to resist telling funny stories about your Chief. But Olga is as close as an oyster. I must have another go at her before my leave comes to an end.'

Sophia was very much nettled by the unfairness of all this. Had she told a single funny story about her Chief? Had she not been a counter-spy for a whole day without hinting a word of it to anybody? Of course, she had been about to take Rudolph into her confidence; now nothing would induce her to do so. She would pay him out for being so horrid to her. Besides he must be broken of this new predilection for Olga; it was becoming a bore.

'Yes, do,' she said; 'have another go at her. Have it now, won't you—much more convenient for me actually because I want to dine with Heatherley.'

'Heatherley? You don't mean Egg? You don't mean that fearful red-headed brute who told us what the President said? Darling Sophia—besides, you're dining with me, you said you would. I haven't seen you for weeks.'

'Darling, I'm terribly sorry, but I haven't seen Heth all day and there are masses of things I want to talk over with him.'

Rudolph said no more. He stopped the cab, got out into the street, told the man to go on to Granby Gate, hailed another cab going in the opposite direction, jumped into it and disappeared.

Sophia minded rather. She had been pleased to see Rudolph, and excited at the idea of spending an evening with him, more pleased and more excited even than she generally was when she had been separated from him for some time, but he must be taught a lesson. It was quite bad enough for him not to say that he was coming on leave, and to let her find him sitting at the Ritz with Olga. But to have him comparing her in a denigrating manner with that pseudo-Muscovite was altogether intolerable. Women are divided into two categories: those who can deal with the men they are in love with, and those who cannot. Sophia was one of those who can.

When she arrived at her house she found a merry meeting of the Brotherhood was in full and joyous progress. Brothers and Sisters were overflowing from all the reception rooms, and the downstairs lavatory was in constant use. A large photograph of Brother Bones was propped up on the drawing-room piano with a bunch of lilies in front of it, for it was the Brother's birthday. Sophia hurried into the lift, and going to the top floor she got the key of her bedroom from Elsie, who had instructions always to lock it on these occasions against the quiet-timers. Sophia had a very hot bath and changed her clothes. Then she went to look for Heth. It was rather a long search, ending in the coal-hole where he was in earnest converse with one of the thin-haired young ladies. Being members of the Brotherhood they were, of course, not at all abashed at being found in such curious circumstances; they merely showed their gums.

Sophia beckoned to Heatherley and whispered in his ear, 'There will be dinner for two in my small sitting-room in about half an hour. I hope you will join me there.'

Heatherley accepted at once. There was always, at these meetings, a large brotherly buffet-meal in the dining-room for which the food was always ordered by Florence, was cold, of the fork variety, non-alcoholic, and very dull. Sophia had an exquisite cook and a pretty taste in food herself, and Luke's wine was not to be sniffed at.

Exactly at the appointed time Heatherley tried the door of the small sitting-room. It was locked. Sophia knew all about the Brothers by now. They would come into her room, and brightly assuring her that she did not disturb them, begin an all-in wrestling match with their souls. She had told Florence that meetings could only take place at 98 Granby Gate, on condition that the Brothers were neither to use the lift nor be guided to force open any doors which they might find locked.

Heatherley announced himself, upon which Sophia let him in. Dinner was waiting on a hot plate, and they helped themselves. Sophia thought he looked like Uriah Heap, and wished she had a more attractive counter-spy to work with, somebody, say, like the ruthless young German in *The Thirty-Nine Steps*; it was impossible to take much pleasure in the company of Heth. How fortunate she loved her work for its own sake (and that of Olga).

With an alluring smile she gave him some soup.

'What was agony 22 for?' she said.

'I don't know what you're talking about.'

'The word, or letters, or code, or whatever it was you wrote on my egg, of course. I took ages trying to decode it, and I wondered if I had the right solution.'

127

'On your egg?' Heatherley put down his soup-spoon and looked completely blank.

'Yes, yes. Think. Of course it must have been you. This morning I had a boiled egg for breakfast, and written on the shell, in pencil, it had agony 22.'

'Sophia, now, why would I write on your egg when I could so easily call you, come round and see you, or leave a note for you here?'

Why indeed? Sophia felt that she had been a fool.

'Well, you said that we must be so careful, that our letters would be opened, and our telephone tapped——'

'If your telephone can be tapped, so could your egg be. No, Sophia, we need to be very, very careful, but there's no sense in writing on eggs, no sense at all, when we can meet all we want to both at the Post and in this house.'

'Anyway, what is our next move? I want to start work,' said Sophia, to change the painful subject.

'I was just coming to that.' Heatherley paused and seemed to consider her. 'How are your nerves?' he said. 'Pretty good? Fine. I have a very delicate job that I wish to entrust to you, delicate, and it may be dangerous. Are you game?'

'Oh, yes, Heatherley, I think so.'

'O.K. Well, presently, when you have quite finished your dinner, I want you to go back to the Post.'

Sophia was not pleased. She had spent eight hours in the Post that day, and had left, as she always did, with a feeling of immense thankfulness and relief. The idea of going back there after dinner did not appeal to her at all.

Heatherley went on, 'You are to make a list of all the nurses there on night duty. Then I want a copy of every word that is written on the notice-board. When you have done that, go to the Regal Cinema and pin an envelope containing the copy to the second stall in the third row on the left-hand side of the centre gangway. You can give me the list of the nurses to-morrow; that is less important. One last word of instruction—on no account take a taxi, that might be fatal. You will be safe enough if you walk it.'

'Well, really,' said Sophia, 'that is far sillier than writing on eggs. Why can't whoever is going to the third stall in the second row walk into the Post and see for himself what is written on the notice-board?'

'Sophia.' Heatherley gave a fish-like look which for a moment, and until she remembered it was only old Heth, quite struck a chill into her heart. 'Are you, or are you not going to help me in clearing out a nest of dangerous spies? Let me tell you that Florence communicates with the rest of her gang by means of that notice-board. My friend cannot go to the Post himself, it would be as much as his life is worth to venture near it. If I were seen to be in communication with him, I too would have short shrift, but it is of vital importance that he should know what is on the board to-night. I can't get away from this Brotherhood meeting without arousing Florence's suspicions, but I thought I had seen a way of fixing things. I thought you would go for me.'

'Oh, all right, Heth, I will. I only meant it sounded rather silly, but I see now that it has to be done. Have some apple flan.'

Chapter Eleven

Now although Sophia supposed herself to be such a keen and enthusiastic spy, she had not really the temperament best suited to the work. It was not in her nature, for instance, to relish being sent out on a cold and foggy evening, after she had had her bath and changed her clothes, in order to do an apparently pointless job for somebody who could quite well do it for himself. Obviously if Heatherley could be closeted for ages in the coal-hole, if he could dine for more than an hour behind a locked door, he could easily escape from the house without Florence or anybody else noticing that he had gone, and do his own dreary work. So she determined that somehow or another she would wriggle out of going, but of course without annoying her Chief as she had not the least intention of being excluded from the delights of counter-espionage, and this might well happen should she be caught out disobeying orders. Sophia was very good at not doing things she disliked, and soon her plans were laid. She remembered that, exasperated by her long and unequal struggle with the overalls, she had herself, that very evening, written out a notice to the effect that those nurses who wanted to have their overalls sorted when they came back from the wash, should write their names clearly both on the overalls themselves and on their pigeon-holes so that Sophia should know where to put them. When she had pinned this to the board, there had been no other notice there, and she had been particularly pleased, thinking that more attention would be paid to it on this account. Now a notice written out by Sophia could not, in the nature of things, contain Florence's secret instructions to her corps of spies. Sophia therefore decided that she would explain to Heatherley that there had been nothing on the notice-board; impossible to make a copy of nothing, so she had done no more about it. That disposed of the notice-board. As for the list of nurses on night duty, she could find that out from Sister Wordsworth's ledger in the morning. And in order to make perfectly certain of not seeing Heatherley before she arrived at the Post she decided to go immediately after breakfast to Phyllis Earle and have her hair done.

As soon as she had reached these comfortable decisions, and with the prospect now of a delicious evening with *Caroline of England* in her warm bed, she became extremely nice, indeed almost flirtatious to Heatherley during the rest of their meal together. When it was over, and Heth had enjoyed brandy and a huge cigar (unlike Florence he did not despise his creature comforts at all), she went upstairs most cheerfully, put on her fur coat with its pretty, scarlet-lined hood, and then was shepherded by a quite unusually genial Heth, through a few Brothers who had finished eating, to the front door.

'I'm afraid it's rather foggy,' he said, peering out with his pale eyes into a solid curtain of fog.

'All the better. I am less likely to be followed,' said Sophia.

'And cold.'

'Ssh. Think of our cause, dear Heatherley.'

'You understand that on no account must you take a taxi,' he reminded her. A more competent spy, she thought, would have seen the impossibility of walking more than two steps in her high-heeled velvet sandals. Anyhow, what did the man think she was, for heaven's sake, a marathon walker?

'No taxi, no indeed.' She stepped gaily into the fog.

'Sophia, you're wonderful.'

'No! No! Good-bye! Good-bye!'

Heatherley shut the front door. Sophia waited a moment and then she went down the area steps, let herself in at the back door and took off her shoes. The servants were in the servants' hall with the wireless blazing away, the back-stairs were pitch dark, and Sophia, using her torch, crept up them and hoped that she would not fall over Heatherley and his girl friend, quiet-timing. They could hardly have got there yet, she thought. On the first floor a door led from the back-stairs into the ballroom, a room which was used about twice a year for parties, and otherwise kept shut up, with dust sheets. She was rather surprised to notice, through the cracks of the door, that the lights were on. Wonderful how the quiet-timers seep into everything. She crept to the door and looked through the keyhole. What she saw turned her to stone.

In a group quite near the door stood Florence, Heatherley, Winthrop, a microphone, and Sir Ivor King, the Lieder König.

'I reckon,' Heatherley was saying, 'that she will be

gone an hour at the very least, in this fog. Five minutes to the Post, ten minutes to copy out the notices, three-quarters of an hour to the Regal and back. And this is a very conservative estimate, I may add, for the fog is thick outside, and I have not allowed for her stopping to talk to anybody at the Post. So you see there is no danger, and we have ample time for everything. If the servants should happen to hear us, they will only think we have switched on the radio and old Ivor is coming over the air better than usual. But they will surely be listening to him themselves downstairs.'

Florence was looking cross. 'I still think it was perfectly stupid of you to tell her anything at all.'

'Say, we've talked all this over before, haven't we? She was wise to everything already, and it was a choice between making her think she was in on the racket, or taking her for a ride. If we had adopted the latter course, the police would have been rubbering round this house and the First Aid Post, and we should have been in a regular spot. Another thing, how would I have got her away this evening if she hadn't been told the works, or some of them—as it is she's just eating out of my hand, will do anything I order her to.'

'Yes, there's something in that,' said Florence grudgingly.

'I tell you,' Heth continued, 'I shall be glad when this business is over and we can do a bunk. I'm not so wild about the inspection of the drain to-night; it may mean they are on to something, or it may be just a routine affair. Either way, I don't like it.'

'In one minute it will be a quarter of,' said Winthrop.

He took up a position in front of the microphone, gazing at his wrist-watch. The others fell silent.

'Germany calling, Germany calling,' Winthrop said, with a very slight German accent and in an entirely different voice from his usual one. 'Here is the Lieder König who is going to give you one of his inimitable programmes of Song Propaganda, so popular with lovers of song and also with lovers of propaganda the world over. The Lieder König.'

Sir Ivor stepped smartly to the microphone. Sophia saw that, out of deference no doubt to the taste of his employers, he was wearing an Aryan wig of metallic brilliance; each curl was like a little golden spring. He raised his voice in song, 'Kathleen Mavourneen the Grey Dawn is breaking,' then he gave a short news bulletin, during the course of which he exactly described that evening's Low cartoon, and also reminded his listeners that Sir Kingsley Wood was due to visit three aerodromes in Yorkshire the following day.

Then Winthrop spoke. 'The Lieder König thinks you would like to know certain facts which have come our way recently. In your great, free, British Empire, in the colony of Kenya, to be exact, there are two honest, thrifty, industrious German farmers, Herr Bad and Herr Wangel. These worthy men have been dragged away from their homes, for no better reason than that they were German-born, and put into the local prison. The prison is a wretched hut, the beds in it are unbearably hard, and the central heating hardly works at all. The prisoners are only allowed baths twice a week. But the worst scandal is the food which is offered to these

Germans. Let me read out the bill of fare, considered by your Government as being sufficient for two grown men.

'Breakfast. A liquid supposed to be coffee, some milk substitute, two lumps of beet sugar, pseudo-eggs and a loaf of brackish bread.

'Luncheon. A so-called veal and ham pie, things which look like potatoes and beans, crab-apple pudding, cheese which is full of mites.

'Tea. Tea (a nerve tonic indispensable to the decadent English, but which we Germans despise).

'Dinner. A thin soup, fish, which is well known in these parts to cause leprosy. The leg of some sheep which had had to be killed, turnips and beetroot such as one feeds to cattle.

'There was no tin of biscuits by their beds in case they woke up hungry in the night.

'When you hear that things like this can happen in your great, vaunted, rich Empire perhaps you will demand that your statesmen, who can allow two honest and unoffending farmers to be so treated, should stop worrying over the scum of Polish cities in luxurious concentration camps, and should be a little bit more concerned about the beam in their own eye, for a change.

'Ask Mr. Churchill, where is the *Ark Royal*?

'Here is the Lieder König again.'

'Well,' said Sir Ivor, 'I hope you have all been as much shocked as I have by the brutal ill-treatment of Herr Bad and Herr Wangel. And now I am going to sing an old favourite, "Under the Deodar".'

He did so, and wound up his programme with 'Fearful the Death of the Diver Must Be, walking alone, walking alone, walking alone in the Dehehehe-he-he-pths of the Sea,' a song of which both he and his admirers were extremely fond, as, at the word 'depths', his voice plumbed hitherto uncharted ones, and any seals or hippos who might happen to be around would roar in an agony of appreciation. 'Good night, dears,' said the old König, 'keep your hairs on. By the way, where *is* the *Ark Royal*?'

'This ends,' said Winthrop, resuming his place at the microphone, 'our programme of Song-Propaganda in English, arranged and sung by the Lieder König.

'Here are the Reichsender Bremen, stations Hamburg and D x B, operating on the thirty-one metre band. I have a special announcement for my English listeners. There will be a Pets' Programme to-morrow from station D x B at 9.30 Greenwich mean time.'

'Now we must scram,' said Heatherley, 'we can always wait in the Maternity Ward if the drain inspection is not finished.'

They all, including the old gentleman, began to struggle into anti-gas clothing. Sophia waited no longer. She flew upstairs to her bedroom and locked herself in, dumbfounded by what she had seen.

Her mind was in a whirl. If Heatherley, who pretended to be an American counter-spy, was really a German spy, perhaps the 'King of Song' was pretending to be a German spy, but was really an English counter-spy? Was he in the pay of the gang, or merely hoaxing them; was he perhaps longing, but unable, to get a message through to the outside world or was he only too anxious that his shameful secret should be kept?

Was he neither spy nor counter-spy, but just a poor old gentleman who got a taste of the thumbscrew twice a day? She wondered, irrelevantly, whether he had seen in the newspapers the pæans of praise followed by the dirges of disillusionment which had so prominent a place in them. Suddenly she remembered that advertisement in *The Times*: 'Poor old gentleman suffering from malignant disease would like to correspond with pretty young lady.' Perhaps he did want to correspond with the pretty young lady, perhaps in fact, it was he who had written on her egg 'Agony (column, box) 22', and who had sent in the advertisement. But if he could do all this, surely he could equally well write to her, to Rudolph, or even to poor Fred directly.

Sophia felt that life had become very complicated all of a sudden. She wished she were more versed in the intricacies of spying, and she very much wished that she could remember more about what had happened in the limited number of spy stories which she had read at various times (generally, of course, on journeys, and how often does one remember anything read on journeys?) At what stage, for instance, does the beautiful heroine abandon her lone trail and call in the heavy hand, large boots and vacant faces of The Yard? She rather thought not until the whole plot had been brilliantly unmasked, except for a few unimportant details, by the glamorous amateur spy herself. This was a point of view which appealed to Sophia, who had to consider Rudolph and Olga as well as King and Country. She went to sleep, having decided on a policy of watchful waiting.

The next day, when Sophia arrived at her First Aid Post, she found an atmosphere of subdued but horrified excitement. She immediately concluded that something untoward had happened at the Theatre; the nurses were always retailing awful atrocities they had witnessed there, and by Theatre they did not at all mean, as anybody else would have, the play; the 'He' of these entertainments was not Tom Walls, but the Surgeon, the 'She' not Hermione Baddeley but the Patient; in short, 'the Theatre' was not the Gaiety but St. Anne's Hospital Operating Theatre. The dramas enacted there alternated, as at the Grand Guignol in Paris, between gruesome tragedy and roaring farce. Sophia supposed that a dead man must have come to life; the reverse, which too often happened, could never have caused such a stir.

Nurses were standing about in little groups, whispering, their eyes as round as marbles. Even Sister Wordsworth and Mr. Stone, whom Sophia found in the office, were looking quite concerned.

'Don't tell Lady Sophia, she wouldn't like it,' said kind Sister Wordsworth, remembering about the knees.

'What?' said Sophia. 'But of course you must tell me. I am so curious, I have the most curious nature in the world. If you don't tell, I shan't get a wink of sleep, or give you one minute's peace until you have. So please, dear Sister Wordsworth.'

Of course they were dying to tell her really. It seemed that, during the drain inspection of the previous night, something too horrible had been found down there, brought up, carried through the Post (dripping, my dear, the smell), and taken to the Hospital mortuary. Sophia began to guess what this object might be, and sure enough, it was the body of a young woman, bound and gagged, and with its face completely gnawed away by rats. Greta.

'But how on earth could it have got there?' she asked, in a shaking voice.

'Why, poor Lady Sophia looks as white as a sheet. I told you we shouldn't tell her. Sit down here, my dear, and have a cup of tea.'

'They say it must have been washed down from much higher up. Nothing to do with this place at all.'

'I should hope not indeed,' said Sophia. 'We should never get another outside patient for practices if they thought they were going to be popped down the main drain when we had finished with them.'

'Outside patient—what an idea. Whatever made you think of that? Well, here's your tea, drink it up, and you'll feel better. We all think it was so clever of Miss Edwards, the way she saw something queer under our feet. I'm longing to have my fortune done again, now that there isn't any more.'

Sophia, however, was beginning to think that there was something very queer indeed, no less a thing than the headquarters of Florence's gang and the hide-out of Sir Ivor King himself; otherwise, why did they hold their broadcast in her ballroom on the night of the drain-inspection? Why did they all work so assiduously at the Post? She had seen a plan of the hospital and knew that underneath the garage there were vast cellars and tunnels, as well as the main drain, no doubt ad-

mirably suited to Florence's purpose. A more convenient place, in fact, it would be hard to imagine, a
place where people wander in and out at all hours, often
bandaged and on stretchers, or disguised in the sinister
uniform of the decontamination squad. Could anything
be more ideal? Then if, for any reason, the Post became
temporarily unsuitable for their purposes, as it had done
the previous evening during the drain inspection, they
could repair, with their old ally (or victim) to Granby
Gate, and under the guise of Brothers could hold their
meetings and conduct their broadcasts there. Florence
might not be a glamour girl, but she seemed to be a
most efficient spy. Sophia hoped that this would all be
a lesson to Luke, and that he would, in future, investigate the antecedents of his soulmates before introducing
them into the home.

Chapter Twelve

LUKE wrote an extremely entertaining letter from America. The change of scene had evidently done him good; he appeared to be in high spirits, and to have cast off the gloom in which he had been enveloped before leaving England.

He said that, having always heard from Mary Pencill that America was the one truly democratic country in the world, quite free from class distinction of any kind, it had seemed to him rather odd that the talk should run almost entirely on such subjects as how charming the late Lady Fort William used to be. 'Another topic which is nearly always introduced, sooner or later, is what do the English think of America? When I reply that, although most Englishmen have heard of America, not one in ten actually believes in it, they seem almost incredulous.' He also said that they were quite indignant at what seemed to them to be the boring progress of the war, and that on the whole, he thought, they hoped that Germany would win. They hoped this, of course, in the kind of irresponsible, guilty way a child hopes the house will catch fire. 'They have a juvenile point of view and in particular an extreme love of sensation.' He had nearly finished his work, he said, and would soon be home. Had had an interesting time, but was looking forward to being back in England again; he would be flying home by clipper. No mention of Florence, Herr

Hitler, or the Brotherhood, and in fact Luke's journey to the New World would seem to have readjusted his perspective as regards the Old.

The news that her husband's return was imminent put an altered complexion on things for Sophia, who realized that she must hurry up with her unmasking activities. Luke was already much disliked owing to his well-known sympathies of the last few years, and it would be extremely awkward for him if a nest of spies were to be found lodged in his house while he himself was there. If, on the other hand, they were tracked down and handed over to justice, by means of the great brilliance and deep cunning of his wife while he was engaged in work of national importance abroad, it would be quite a different affair, and could reflect only to his credit.

Sophia decided that she must immediately find out where the King of Song was hiding, or being hidden, and get into communication with that treacherous and venal (or, alternatively, loyal and disinterested) old body. She felt that even if the former adjectives proved to be correct, he would not have lost all his affection for his godchild; she could not somehow imagine him handing her over to Heatherley, the drain and thumbscrew. If really on the side of England all along, he would be only too glad to be assisted from the clutches of his captors. She hoped he would not prove to be drugged, like Van der Lubbe, but supposed that he would hardly be in such good voice if so. The more she thought of it, the more she felt certain that he must be underneath the First Aid Post, and that one clue to his whereabouts lay in the snacks which Florence and Heatherley carried from the canteen in such quantities. Their appetites had become quite a joke with the nurses. The maternity ward was too small to hide a mouse, but next door to that was the hospital museum, a huge, half dark vault, of a most sinister shape and size. The manhole which led to the main drain was in Mr. Stone's little office, so they would not be able to use that; investigation, she felt, should be made in the museum.

She also decided that it was no longer possible for her to blaze a lone trail through the jungle of spies and counter-spies that her life had now become. After all, she had a lot of valuable counter-espionage work to her credit; the brilliant piece of feminine intuition which had prevented her from leaving the house on Heather-ley's bogus errand, as many a lesser woman might have done, having led to the sensational discoveries that the King of Song was still in this country, that Heatherley Egg, far from being a counter-spy, was a counter-counter-spy, and that Winthrop, if not Heatherley himself, was a German. In *The Thirty-Nine Steps*, even Scudder, who, like her, preferred to work on his own, had finally bequeathed his little black notebook to an accomplice; Sophia had no black notebook: all the more necessary that she should have an accomplice. At any moment she might be drained, and then nobody would ever know that she had been a beautiful female spy all along. It was a dreadful prospect.

The choice of an accomplice lay between Fred and Rudolph, and while Rudolph probably had more initiative and more spare time at present, she really

143

favoured Fred on account of his being so much more under her thumb. There was quite good reason, knowing what she did of Fred's character, to hope that in his eyes she would be the Chief; Fred was used to Chiefs, and in fact had never yet been without one during the whole of his life. Rudolph, as she very well knew, would order her about or ignore her, just as it suited him; besides, it would give her the most intense pleasure, as well as serving him right for flirting with Olga, to leave Rudolph out of all this until she could point to the fruits of her activities in the shape of at least three prisoners in the Tower. Having therefore, quite decided upon Fred, to the point of lifting the receiver of her telephone to ring him up, she suddenly remembered the main drain and the possible fate of inept counter-spies. Fred had a young and lovely wife who seemed to be devoted to the idea of him; he also had two fat babies. Rudolph had nothing but a perfectly horrible sister who had often been very rude to Sophia. She rang up Rudolph.

Rudolph was by now bored to death with Olga and her long stories about a job and a Chief that too palpably did not exist. On the other hand, she having been the cause of his break with Sophia, he had felt himself obliged to haunt her company. When he realized that he was being summoned back into the fold he made no secret of his delight.

'Serge came round this morning to horse-whip me,' he said; 'wasn't it fascinating? It seems that he bought a horse-whip at Fortnum's on Olga's account, and he turned up here with it very early, about nine. He hadn't been to bed at all (there's a new place called The Nuthouse, we'll go to-night). The porter telephoned up to my room and said, "There's a gentleman in sporting kit, wants to see you most particular," so I had him sent up with my breakfast, and in comes old Voroshilov, furling and unfurling a great whip; I felt quite giddy. So I ordered some drinks and he sat on my bed and told me that Olga bumps up his allowance every time he horse-whips anybody for making a pass at her, because she read somewhere that this was the form in Imperial Russia. Then he told me all about his Blossom. He simply loved his Blossom, apparently he never loved any other creature so much in his life. He says it was grossly unfair, the way they dismissed him; he only passed out because she passed out first and he couldn't think of anything else to do, with her lying there so flat and dead looking, and the idea of her being in the charge of poor Fred makes him quite sick. I should think he feels quite sick, quite often actually, because he is busy drinking himself to death—he was, anyway, of course, so it doesn't make all that difference. Still, it's rather dreadful to see the poor old tartar so sad and low; he used to be such a jolly old drunk, but he was crying like anything; he has only just gone. When do I see you, shall I come round now or meet you at the Post?'

'No, neither. I don't want to be seen seeing you, you see.'

'Why ever not?'

'Well, I can't explain for the present.'

'Good heavens, Sophia, is Luke cutting up rough?'

'Luke's not back yet, and you know quite well he

never cuts up rough. I will meet you at the Ritz in half an hour.'

'You'll be seen seeing me there all right. However,' said Rudolph quickly, not wishing her, as in her present eccentric mood she easily might, to change her mind, 'meet you there, darling; good-bye.'

Sophia smiled to herself. That evening spent with Heatherley instead of with Rudolph had been wonderfully productive of results, one way and another.

When she arrived at the Ritz, Rudolph was already there reading an early edition of an evening paper. He stood up to greet her, hardly raising his eyes from the paper. Sophia sat down beside him, then, remembering what she was, she bobbed up again in order to see that nobody was lurking behind her chair and that there was no microphone underneath it.

'Walking round your chair for luck?' said Rudolph, still reading.

'Put that paper down, darling. I've got a very great deal to tell you.'

'Go ahead.'

'Stop reading, then.'

'I can read and listen to you quite well.'

'Probably you can. But I can't talk to you while you're reading. Darling, really you are rude. You might have been married to me for years.'

'To all intents and purposes I have.'

'That's very rude, too. Thank heavens I have Luke to fall back on.'

'Poor old Luke. You always talk about him as if he were a lie-low.'

'So he is, and it's a jolly nice thing to be. The more I see of you, the more I like Luke, as somebody said about dogs. Rudolph now, please don't let's quarrel. Put that paper down and talk to me.'

Rudolph did so with bad grace. They were both by now thoroughly out of temper with each other.

'Well, what is it?'

'Darling, now listen. You know about me being beautiful?'

'You're all right.'

'No, Rudolph, please say I'm beautiful; it's part of the thing.'

'I suppose you're going to tell me you're a beautiful female spy?'

'In a way, I was.'

'Yes, I'm quite sure you were. And that you have a Chief, but you don't feel happy about his loyalty, so you're really working on your own, and the War Office and Scotland Yard haven't got an inkling of what you're up to because you're blazing a lone trail, but soon there will be sensational revelations, and you will be a national heroine. Oh God! women are bores in wars.' Rudolph returned to his paper.

Sophia left the Ritz in a great temper, and went straight to her Post where she had lunch alone at the canteen. It was much too late now to ring up Fred; he would be with his Blossom; she would have to make investigations on her own after all.

Chapter Thirteen

SOPHIA had wondered why the canteen was so empty, and when she got downstairs she found the reason was that the Post was in the throes of a major practice. This event had been canvassed with great excitement for the past few days, and nothing but Sophia's preoccupation with other matters could have put it out of her mind. As soon as she arrived, she was engulfed in it. Not only did the Southern Control hiss into her ear 'Practice red, expect casualties', not only did casualties covered with 'wounds' of the most lugubrious description appear in shoals—these things had often happened before and been regarded as part of everyday work—to-day was made memorable by the fact that a real (not practice) Admiral was scheduled to escort a real (not practice) Royal Princess round the Post to see it at work.

Sophia immediately saw that if she was ever going to conduct investigations, this would be the time. Heatherley and Winthrop were on continual stretcher duty and would not be able to leave the Treatment Room for a moment, except to carry 'cases' upstairs to the Hospital. Only Florence was unemployed; this must be remedied. Sophia went into the Treatment Room in search of Sister Wordsworth. It was a hive of industry; dressings and splints were laid out in quantities, and the instruments were all getting a double dose of sterilization, as though the royal eye were fitted with a microscopic lens which would enable it to note, with disapproval, fast gathering clouds of streptococci. Sister Wordsworth stood surveying the scene.

Sophia said, 'Can I speak to you a moment?' and suggested that if everything was supposed to be in progress exactly as though there had been a real raid, surely Florence ought to be sent a practice pregnancy. Sister Wordsworth saw the force of this argument, and taking hold of the next woman 'patient' who appeared, she bundled her into the Labour Ward.

'Sixty-five if she's a day,' she said in a loud cheerful aside. 'I should think it will be a very difficult delivery. Have the forceps handy, Sister Turnbull, and plenty of hot water.' Florence looked very peevish indeed, and prepared to do as she was told with a bad grace.

At this moment the real Princess appeared, and jokes were forgotten.

As soon as H.R.H. had seen her office, and gone through into the Treatment Room, Sophia summoned up all her courage and left her chair by the telephone. If it rang while she was gone, Sister Wordsworth would never forgive her; this would have to be risked, among other things. She ran down a back passage to the hospital museum. The door was locked but she had Sister Wordsworth's master-key, with which she opened it. Florence was standing in the Labour Ward, the door of which was at right angles to that of the Museum; she appeared to be leaning over her aged victim, and her back was turned on Sophia who slipped into the Museum carefully, shutting the door behind her. Then, shaking with terror, she switched on her electric torch and crept down the main avenue between the glass cases. She passed the pre-natal Siamese twins, fearful little withered white figures, unnaturally human and with horrible expressions of malignity on their faces. She passed the diseased hearts and decayed livers, and reached the case of brains with tumours on them. Then her heart stood still. On the floor beneath the brains, shining in the light of her torch like a golden wire, was a springy butter-coloured curl which could only have come from one source. The horrified curiosity felt by Robinson Crusoe when he saw the footstep of Man Friday, the ecstasy and joy of Mme. Curie when at last she had a piece of radium, were now experienced with other and more complex sensations by Sophia. For a minute or two she almost choked with excitement; then, recovering herself, she followed in the direction in which (so far as a curl can be said to point) it pointed. Under the large intestines another one winked out a welcome, under the ulcerated stomachs was a third. The passage ended with a case of bladders against the wall, and under this was a curl. Very gingerly Sophia pushed the case. It moved. She put down her torch and lifted the case away from the wall. Behind it there was a door. As she opened this door she knew that she must be the bravest woman in the world. As a child, if she had been extremely frightened of something, she used to remind herself that she was descended from Charles II, and this had sustained her. She now invoked this talisman, to but little avail. The Merry Monarch had lived too long ago, and blankets the adult Sophia knew to have more than one side. In any case, even if his blood did flow in her veins, she thought, the worst terrors he had faced were Roundheads and death on the block, or, later in life, highwaymen who would have been easily charmed by a guinea and a royal joke. A hospital museum with its grisly exhibits, the darkness, the main drain, possible rats and creeping spies, were a test of nerves which might well break down the resistance of a man far braver than Charles II had ever shown himself to be.

She was now faced by a long flight of stone stairs leading, she supposed, to some fearful dungeons. She went down them, and then down a short passage at the end of which was another door which she opened. Sitting in quite a cheerful little room with an electric fire was the old gentleman himself.

'Darling,' he cried, 'what has happened—are they all caught? How did you get here? Where are the police?'

'Ssh,' said Sophia, her knees turning to jelly. 'I am all alone. I came down from the Post.'

'But my darling child, this is terrible, so terribly dangerous. You must go back at once. But just listen carefully to me. They—(do you know who I mean, Florence and the others?)'

Sophia nodded. 'Yes, I know about them being spies; go on.'

'They have got some scheme on foot which I must find out. They are putting it into execution next Friday, in three days' time. It is something devilish; I have half guessed what, but I must know for certain. Apart from that, I know everything about the German spies in this country. Now I want you to tell the police where I am and all about Florence and Co., so that they can be watched. But I also want them to wait before rounding up the gang until six o'clock on Friday evening. It, whatever it is, will happen at ten o'clock that night, so if I don't know all by six, I probably never shall. Anyhow, I don't dare leave it until later. Now quickly go back. If they find you here they will put us both in the main drain, and all my work will have been wasted. Go, go. Be careful now. Good-bye till we meet again, my dearest. Good-bye.'

Something in the old King's manner terrified Sophia. He looked at her, she thought, as if he never expected to see her again in life; he spoke with the abruptness and irritation of a badly frightened man. She turned and fled back, up the stairs to the museum; here, with shaking hands, she put back the case of bladders as she had found it against the door. Then she crept through the medical curiosities and out again into the Post. The door of the Labour Ward was shut this time and the coast seemed clear. She ran as fast as she could to the office, collapsed into her chair and felt extremely faint; she held her head between her knees for a few moments until the giddiness had passed off. She longed for brandy, which she knew to be unobtainable.

The Royal inspection was still in progress; indeed, although it seemed to her like several days, Sophia had only been away from the office for ten minutes, and very fortunately the telephone bell had not rung once during this time. It did so now, 'Southern Control speaking, practice white.' Sophia decided that she was not temperamentally suited to the profession, which she had so gaily chosen, of secret agent; she was not nearly brave enough. Her teeth were still chattering, her hand was trembling so much that she could hardly lift the telephone receiver. She would blaze her lone trail no longer, that evening the whole affair was going to be placed before Scotland Yard, and her responsibility would be at an end. This comforting resolution greatly strengthened her nerves; a large, red-faced policeman would be more stimulating than brandy and she would insist on having one to watch over her until Friday. She wondered if she could persuade him to sleep in her bathroom, and thought that nothing could give her so much happiness.

Sister Wordsworth now made a cheerful reappearance, having just seen the Princess out to her car. She said that everything had gone off perfectly. Sister Turnbull's patient, it seemed, had come through her dangerous and unusual experience as easily as if she had been twenty instead of sixty (twin boys, Neville and Nevile, after the Blue Book), and was now with all the other patients enjoying a nice cup of tea in the canteen. The Princess had been charming and had amazed everybody, royal persons always being assumed to be half-witted, deaf and dumb until they have given practical proof to the contrary, by asking quite intelligent questions. The Admiral had winked at several of the nurses, and had been bluff, honest-to-God, hearty and all other things that are expected of seafaring men. In the short, everybody had been pleased and put into a satisfied frame of mind, and the Post rang with the rather loud chatter which is induced by great relief from strain.

Sophia, joining with the others, almost forgot her night-mare experiences in the museum.

When the time came for her to go home, however, she felt that she really could not face the terrors of the black-out and walk, as she generally did. She was feeling frightened again, and the idea of masked men waiting to boo out at her from behind sandbags was too un-nerving. So she telephoned for a taxi. As she got into it, she wondered whether she really ought to go straight to Scotland Yard before going home. After some hesitation she decided that she felt too tired and dirty. Dinner and especially a bath were necessary before she could under-take such an expedition; besides, it was quite possible that she might even persuade some fatherly inspector to go and see her, in comfort, at Granby Gate, which would be much nicer.

She took a whisky and soda to her bedroom, un-dressed slowly before the fire, and wrapped herself in her dressing-gown; then she sat for a time sipping the whisky. She felt very much restored, and presently went to turn on her bath. Sitting on the edge of it was Heatherley.

Sophia huddled into her dressing-gown, paralysed with terror. She had a remote feeling of thankfulness that she had put on the dressing-gown; as her bathroom led out of her bedroom and had no other entrance she very often did not. Heatherley had an extremely dis-agreeable, not to say alarming expression on his face, and she was far too much unnerved to reproach him for being in her bathroom, or indeed to say anything.

He stood up and barked at her, and any doubts left in her mind as to his being a German were removed.

154

'You were seen this afternoon, coming out of the Hospital Museum. What were you doing there?'

Sophia felt like a rabbit with a snake. 'Oh, nothing much,' she said. 'I always think those Siamese twins are rather little duckies, don't you?'

She saw that this had teased Heatherley and it occurred to her that he did not know about her finding the King of Song. She rather supposed that if he had even guessed at such a thing, she would by now be going for a swim down the drain. 'Pull yourself together, you're descended from Charles II, aren't you?' Sophia was enough of a snob to feel that this equivocal connexion put her on a superior footing to Heatherley whether he was American or German, neither country having, so far as she could remember, existed in Charles II's day. 'Now do you agree,' she babbled on, playing for time, 'that Charles II was far the most fascinating of all our Kings?'

'I'm afraid I have not come here to discuss Charles II. I have come to inform you upon two subjects. First, you should know that I am not, as you supposed, a counter-spy.'

'Hun or Yank?' asked Sophia. A spasm of intense rage crossed Heatherley's face. She was beginning positively to enjoy the interview.

'I am the head of the German espionage system in this country. My name is Otto von Eiweiss. Florence is Truda von Eiweiss, my wife. Heil Hitler.'

'Your wife!' said Sophia, 'goodness me, all this time I've been thinking you fancied her!'

'Secondly,' went on Heth, taking no notice of her but

trembling with anger, 'Truda and I think you know too much. We think you have been prying into affairs which do not concern you. We also think that you might soon begin to prattle of these affairs to your friends, who, although they all belong to that decadent class which we National Socialists most despise, might in their turn (purely by accident, of course, they are too soft and stupid to have any purpose in life) harm us with their talk. So, in order to make certain that none of this shall happen, we have taken your bulldog, Millicent, into protective custody, as we have noticed that in your unnatural English way you seem to love her more than anything else. In three days' time, if you behave exactly as we tell you, she will be back once more under your eiderdown, but otherwise——'

'Quilt,' Sophia corrected him mechanically. She despised the word eiderdown. Then, suddenly realizing what she meant, 'My bulldog, Millicent—— Milly? You fearful brute,' and she forgot all about Charles II and what fun it was to tease Heth, and went for him tooth and nail.

Heatherley warded off her bites and scratches with humiliating ease, and twisting one of her arms in schoolboy fashion, he continued, 'Now, be quite quiet, and listen to me.'

'Ow, this hurts; let me go.'

'Are you going to be quiet? Good. Now I shall continue our little chat. The bulldog, Millicent, as I was just remarking, is in protective custody.'

'Where?'

'I shall not divulge.'

156

'Has she had her dinner at six?'

'If her dinner-time is punctually at six she most probably has. She was removed from your house at six-thirty precisely.'

'Oh! Where is she, please?'

'It is no concern of yours where she is.'

'You brutish hun, of course it is a concern of mine. In this weather. She will catch cold, she will get bronchitis. These dogs have frightfully weak chests. Savage —kaffir—fuzzy-wuzzy—you——'

'To call me all these things will not advance the cause of Millicent, very far from it. She is now in my power, and you had better be nice to me.' Heatherley leant towards her with a horrible leer.

'I shall tell Florence about you coming into my bathroom when I have nearly nothing on,' she said. This shot appeared to have gone home. Heatherley looked quite disconcerted.

'The bulldog,' he said, after a pause, 'will be returned to you in perfectly good condition so long as you have been obedient to us and stuck not only to the letter but also to the spirit of our instructions. Otherwise, I regret to inform you that not only will she be vivisected for several hours and then put, as Greta was put, still alive, into the main drain, but that, long before you can act, you also will have ceased to live.'

'Devil. I must say I shouldn't care to be you, after you are dead. Would you like to hear what will happen to you? Well, you'll lie on a gridiron to eternity and baste —do you hear me, B A S T E.'

'Instead of abusing me, and threatening me with the

157

out-worn superstitions of a decadent religion, it will be better for you to listen to what I have to say.

'For the next three days and nights either Florence, or Gustav, whom you know as Winthrop, or I myself will be watching you like lynxes; you will never be out of the sight of one or other. Florence will take night duty and sleep in your room. Gustav and I will take turns by day. If you make the smallest sign to anybody, or convey any message to the outside world, we shall know it, and within half an hour the bulldog Millicent will be wishing she had never been born.'

'How do you mean Florence will sleep in my room? There's only one bed.'

'It is a very large one. You can take the choice between sharing it with Florence and having another bed made up in your room.'

'Ugh!' Sophia shuddered. Then she rang the bell, and feeling uncommonly foolish, went into her bedroom, where she told Elsie that she had been suffering from nightmares, and that Miss Turnbull had very kindly consented to sleep in her room.

'Oh, and Elsie, tell Mrs. Round that I have taken Milly to the vet, to be wormed, will you? She'll be about three days.'

'Yes, m'lady. We were all wondering where Milly had got to.'

When Elsie had gone, Heatherley came out of the bathroom and said, 'One last word. I warn you that you had better act in good faith. It will not avail you to do such things as, for instance, write notes in invisible ink on match-boxes, for we shall act on the very smallest

158

suspicion. Your telephone here is cut; please do not have it mended. It will be the safest from your point of view, and that of your bulldog, if you were to see nobody at all except the personnel at the Post. Of them, I may tell you that ninety per cent are members of my corps, and will assist in keeping you under observation. Miss Wordsworth received last night in an omnibus a *piqure* that will incapacitate her for a week at least.'

'I see, you are white slavers as well as everything else.'

'Mr. Stone, as you are aware, has gone away on holiday. You will sit alone in the office, and either Gustav or myself will often sit there with you. When you think you are quite alone, one of us will be watching you through a rent in the hessian.'

Sophia lay awake all night. Florence did not, it is true, snore so loudly or so incessantly as Milly, nor was her face so near to Sophia's as Milly's generally became during the course of a night. What she did was to give an occasional rather sinister little 'honk' which was far more disturbing. But in any case Sophia would probably have lost her sleep. There seemed to be no way out of the quandary in which she found herself, look at it how she would. Even supposing that she was anxious to sacrifice Milly to the common good, which she was not, very, it seemed to her that she would only have time to give one hysterical shout before she was herself overpowered, gagged, and put down the drain, or, if in the street, liquidated in some other way. Then her secret, like Scudder's, would die with her, for it was too late now to begin keeping a black notebook. The prospect was discouraging.

She turned about miserably racking her brains until she was called, when the sight of Florence sitting up in bed, and disposing of an enormous breakfast, quite put her off her own. For a moment she forgot her troubles in the fascination of seeing how Florence fixed herself into the stays, but with so many so much weightier affairs on her mind, Sophia hardly got the best advantage from this experience. For one thing she was tortured by wondering who would give Milly her morning run and whether she would do all she should. If she was being kept, like the old gentleman, underneath the Post, there was unlikely to be such a thing as a bit of grass for her, unless some kind of subterranean weed grew beside the main drain. Then there was the question of food.

She had sent Florence to Coventry. Florence, she considered, having lived with her all these months and accepted her fur cape, only to repay by kidnapping Milly, had proved herself to be outside the pale, what Lord Haw-haw calls 'not public school'. Sophia would not and could not speak to her, so she would have to discuss Milly's diet-sheet with Heatherley, and meanwhile she decided that she would take a dinner for her in a parcel when she went to the Post.

She and Florence spent a dismal morning together in Harrods, where, whenever Sophia saw somebody she knew, Florence threatened her with the barrel of a gun which she kept in her bag; after this they went off, still in silence and rather early, to the Post. Sophia was clutching a damp parcel of minced meat which she deposited in the Labour Ward when they arrived, and hoped for the best. She thought it was a gesture rather like that made by primitive Greek peasants who are supposed to put out, in some sacred spot, little offerings of food for the god Pan.

Heatherley's predictions were correct. Sister Wordsworth was off duty, ill, Mr. Stone was away on a week's holiday, and Sophia sat alone in the office. Heatherley and Winthrop took it in turns to watch over her, and the first thing she saw when she came in was a dreadful, unwinking, pale blue eye pressed against a tear in the sacking. There was nothing to be done, nothing whatever. She felt quite sick, and the hours dragged away slowly. Even Macaulay's *History of England* held no more charms for her, the landing of the Prince of Orange among the rude fisher-folk of Torquay with a background of ghostly future villas was a painted scene which could not have much interest for one who sat on such a powder-barrel as she did. The question uppermost in her mind now was 'What is going to happen on Friday?' but the more she thought, the less she could form an opinion. Perhaps it was only that on that day Florence and her corps of spies were leaving the country; she felt, however, that it was something far more sinister. The assassination of some public man, for instance; although it was difficult to think of any public man whose assassination would not greatly advance the Allied cause, and the same objection, multiplied by about twelve hundred, would, of course, apply to blowing up the Houses of Parliament. In Sophia's opinion, this would no longer even be an æsthetic disaster, since they had been subjected to the modish barbarism of pickling.

That evening Fred dined with her, a long-standing engagement. She was told that she could choose which of her three chaperons should attend her on this occasion, and chose Heatherley. He was the one she hated the most, because she was quite certain it was he who had thought of abducting Milly, and she hoped to be able to tease him by talking about Germany with Fred and at him. Unfortunately this did not work out very well. A Fred racked with ideals, and in the grip of Federal Union, was quite a different cup of tea from the old, happy-go-lucky Fred who used to join with her in blasting abroad, its food, its manners, its languages, its scenery, and the horrible time one had getting there.

'I can't see eye to eye with you, my dear Sophia,' he said pompously, when she thought she had worked him up to better things. 'I think of all foreigners, even Germans, in quite a different light now. To me they are our brothers in Union. Whatever happens, don't you see, we must finish the war with a great glow of love in our hearts—the punishment we are giving them should be quite in the spirit of "this hurts me more than it does you".'

Heatherley gave a loathsome snigger.

'I beg your pardon? Of course, Mr. Egg, as you come from the United States of America, you can tell us all about Federal Union from experience. I am sure you must think highly of it?'

'It works very badly over there, and would be quite useless in Europe. In Europe you have one Power so far in advance of all the rest that ethical sense as well as common sense would put the other countries in complete submission to its dictates.'

'Yes, that's what I always say,' said Sophia, 'but, of course, it will be an awful bore having to rule over those fiendish foreigners, and I rather doubt if we can be bothered. Perhaps we could make the French do it for us.'

Heatherley smiled in a superior way. He seemed far too comfortable to please Sophia and she greatly feared that his plans, whatever they were, must be maturing satisfactorily for him. She made no attempt to communicate in any way with Fred, knowing that, quite alone and uninterrupted, it would have taken her a good hour to explain the whole matter to him. Fred liked to get to the bottom of things, to ask a hundred questions and to write a great deal in his notebook; his particular temperament rendered such devices as tapping on his leg in Morse Code (even had Sophia been sufficiently expert to do so) much worse than useless. She very wisely left the whole thing alone.

The evening was not a great success. Fred asked where Milly was, and when told about the vet, reminded Sophia that she and Abbie had been wormed together less than two months before. He went on to tell her what a strain it was on a dog's inside, asking what evidence she had of Milly's worms, until poor Sophia could have screamed. Then they listened to the King of Song, but he was not really much in form. At the end of his programme, however, there was a drop of comfort for Sophia when he sang, very distinctly, 'Milly is my darling, my darling, my darling, Milly is my darling, the young bow wow dear,' after which she heard, or thought she heard, a rumbling snore. If Milly was with the old gentleman that would be nice for both of them, and especially, of course, for the old gentleman. At last Fred took his leave, after which Heatherley escorted Sophia, who was by now very sleepy in spite of all her cares, to join Florence in her bedroom.

This was the end of the first day.

Chapter Fourteen

THE next morning Sophia, having enjoyed from sheer exhaustion, an excellent night's rest, awoke feeling more resolute. She had often heard that the Germans are the stupidest people in the world; when she remembered this and also the fact that, until she had found out that they were spies, she had always looked upon Florence, Heatherley and Winthrop as being the greatest bores she knew, it seemed to her that it should be possible to outwit Truda, Otto and Gustav, even if they were three to one against her. She stayed in bed until it was time to go to St. Anne's, thinking very hard.

Clearly the first thing to be done was to write out a concise report of her situation, and this she must keep handy in case she had an opportunity, unobserved, of giving it to some reliable person. Hatred of Heatherley, even more than fear, lent her courage and cunning, and when she had been at the Post a little while, she put down her handkerchief over a stump of pencil on the table. Presently she picked up both handkerchief and pencil and went off to the lavatory, the only place where she could be out of sight of the unholy trinity, one of whose members followed her to its very door. Here she wrote, very quickly, on her handkerchief, 'Spies. Milly and Ivor King imprisoned below Post. Tell police but act carefully. I am watched. No joke.' She had to waste valuable space and time in saying 'no joke' because she knew that if this missive should happen to reach any of her friends they would be sure to think it was one and act accordingly. The trouble now was to think of somebody to give it to, as, although she felt certain that Heatherley was bluffing when he said that nearly all the nurses were his fellow-spies, she did not know any of them well enough, now that Sister Wordsworth was away, to be positive beyond doubt of their integrity. She thought that if, by the next day, nothing else had turned up, she would, as a last resort, give the handkerchief to one of them; meanwhile she hoped for luck.

The sister in charge of the Treatment Room brought a Mrs. Twitchett into the office. She was one of those fat women whose greatly overpowdered faces look like plasticine, and whose bosoms, if pricked, would surely subside with a loud bang and a gust of air. The sister introduced her to Sophia, saying that she had already been taken on at the local A.R.P. headquarters as a part-time worker for St. Anne's; Sophia's business was to note down all particulars on the card index.

'Emma Twitchett,' she wrote, '144 The Boltons. Qualifications, First Aid, Home Nursing and Gas Certificates. Next of kin, Bishop of the Antarctic. Religion, The Countess of Huntingdon's Connexion.'

Here Sophia looked up sharply and saw, what in her preoccupation had not hitherto dawned on her, that Emma Twitchett was none other than Rudolph. For the first moment of crazy relief she thought that he must know everything and have come to rescue her, Milly and Sir Ivor. Then she realized that this could not be the case. He was merely bored and lonely without her, and was hoping that he would get back into favour by means of an elaborate joke. It was absolutely important to prevent him from giving himself away in the office, while under the impression that they were alone. Sophia was only too conscious of the eye in the hessian. As soon as she had scribbled down Mrs. Twitchett's particulars, she hurried him out into the Post.

Although it could not be said that Sophia had hitherto proved herself to be a very clever or successful counter-spy, she now made up for all her former mistakes by perfectly sensible behaviour. The luck, of which she had been so hopeful, had come her way at last and she did not allow it to slip through her fingers. She conducted Mrs. Twitchett, as she always did new people, round the Post, chatting most amicably. She was careful to omit nothing, neither the rest room upstairs, the canteen, the ladies' cloakroom nor the room with the nurses' lockers. She hoped that Rudolph would notice, and remember afterwards, how Winthrop, without giving himself the trouble to dissimulate his movements, was following them closely during this perambulation. Sophia was only too thankful that it was Winthrop who, she estimated, was about half as intelligent as Heatherley. At last she took Mrs. Twitchett to the exit and showed her out, saying 'Very well then, that will be splendid; to-morrow at twelve. Oh yes, of course,' she said rather hesitatingly and shyly, 'Yes, naturally, Mrs. Twitchett, I'll lend you mine.' She took out her handkerchief and offered it to Rudolph with a smile. 'No, of course, bring it back any time. I have another in my bag; it's quite all right. Good, then, see you to-morrow; that will be very nice. So glad you are coming; we are rather short-handed, you know.'

She went back without even glancing at Winthrop who was hovering about inside the Post, and who followed her to the office. Then she sat for a while at her table trembling very much and expecting that any moment she would be summoned to the drain, but as time went on and nothing had happened, she took up her knitting. If she had a certain feeling of relief that, at any rate, she had been able to take a step towards communication with the outside world, she was also tortured with doubts as to whether Rudolph would ever see what was written on the handkerchief and whether, if he did, he would not merely say that women were bores in wars. Olga had certainly queered the pitch for her rivals in the world of espionage as far as Rudolph was concerned. Also, if he did have the luck to read and the sense to follow her directions, would he be in time? He must hurry; she felt sure that after to-morrow any action which might be taken would be too late to save Milly and the old gentleman, certainly too late to catch Florence. To-morrow was what the posters call zero hour. The rest of that day dragged by even more horribly slowly than the preceding one, and there was no sign from Rudolph. She could not help half expecting that he would have got some kind of a message through to her; when seven o'clock arrived and there was nothing, she was bitterly disappointed. Heatherley conducted her home in a taxi, dined with her and never let her out of his sight until Florence was ready to take charge of her. Sophia did not sleep a single wink; she lay strenuously willing Rudolph to read her handkerchief.

On the morning of the third and last day, Sophia would have been ready to construe anything which seemed at all mysterious into a code message from Rudolph. But nothing of the sort came her way. She eagerly scanned her egg for a sign of calligraphy, however faint; it was innocent, however, of any mark. The agony column of *The Times* was equally unproductive, nor had Milly contributed to the dog advertisements; there was not even a mention of French bulldogs. Her morning post consisted of nothing more hopeful than *Harrod's Food News*. In fact, it became obvious to Sophia that Rudolph had never read her S O S at all, or if he had that he did not believe in it. Two large tears trickled down her cheeks. She decided that if nothing had materialized to show that Rudolph was helping by four o'clock, she would abandon Milly and the old gentleman to death and worse in the main drain, and dash out of the Post on the chance of finding a policeman before she too was liquidated.

Having made up her mind to some definite action, she felt happier. She jumped out of bed, dressed in a great hurry and led poor Florence, who suffered a good deal from fallen arches, round and round Kensington Gardens for two hours at least.

When Sophia arrived at the Post, accompanied by a limping Florence, the first person she saw was Mrs. Twitchett. Her doubts were dispersed in a moment and great was her relief. Rudolph must certainly be working on her side; it would be unnatural for anybody to go to the trouble of dressing up like that, twice, for a joke. Mrs. Twitchett was busily employed in the Labour Ward, but found time, when Sophia came down from her luncheon at the canteen, to go round to the office and give back the borrowed handkerchief. Sophia put it away in her bag without even looking at it.

'So kind of you,' said Mrs. Twitchett. 'I have had it washed and ironed for you, of course. And now you must forgive me if I run back to the Labour Ward. I am in the middle of a most fascinating argument with Sister Turnbull about umbilical cords. Thank you again, very much, for the handkerchief.'

Rudolph's disguise was perfect, and Sophia did not feel at all nervous that Florence would see through it; he had, in his time, brought off much more difficult hoaxes, and she herself had not seen who it was yesterday until he began to make a joke of the card index.

Presently Sophia gave a loud sniff, rummaged about in her bag and pulled out the handkerchief. Rudolph really did seem to have had it washed and ironed, unless it was a new one. Slowly she spread it out, gave it a little shake and blew her nose on it. The letters 'O.K.' were printed in one corner, so that was all right. She began to do her knitting. An almost unnatural calm seemed to have descended on the Post. Several people, as well as Sister Wordsworth, were on the sick list, and the personnel were so depleted that it was not even possible to hold the usual practice in the Treatment Room. The wireless, joy of joys, was out of order. One nurse came in and asked Sophia for a clean overall in which to go to the theatre, and Sophia felt guilty because she had known that this girl's own overall was lost in the wash and she ought to have sent a postcard about it to the laundry. As she got a clean one out of the general store, she assured the girl that she had done so and was eagerly awaiting the reply. It seemed that to-day was to be a gala at the theatre, with two cerebral tumours and a mastoid. This nurse had been looking forward to it all the week. Sophia helped her with her cap, and she dashed away to her treat, singing happily.

Sophia felt very restless, and wandered into the Treatment Room where, done out of the ordinary practice, the nurses, in an excess of zeal, were giving each other bed pans. Further on, in the Labour Ward, Sister Turnbull and Mrs. Twitchett sat on the floor counting over the contents of the poison cupboard. Mrs. Twitchett was enlarging on the most horrid aspects of childbirth. Then Sophia went back to the office, and hour upon hour went by with absolutely nothing happening until she thought she would scream.

Suddenly, just before it was time for her to go off duty, all the lights went out. This was always happening at the Post; nevertheless Sophia found herself under the table before she had time consciously to control her actions. A moment later she heard Winthrop push his way through the sacking curtain and he began to flash a powerful torch round the office, evidently looking for her. In one more minute he must see her. Sophia experienced a spasm of sick terror, like a child playing a too realistic game of hide and seek, and then, almost before she had time to remember that this was no game at all, two more torches appeared in the doorway, and, by the light of Winthrop's which was now flashed on to them, she could see Mrs. Twitchett, accompanied by the reassuring form of a tin-hatted policeman. For a few moments the office resembled the scene of a gangster play in which it is impossible to discover what is happening; however, when the shooting and scuffling was over, she saw Winthrop being led away with gyves upon his wrists, and this gave her great confidence.

'Sophia, where are you?' shouted Rudolph.

Sophia crawled out from under her table feeling unheroic, but relieved.

'Good girl,' he said. 'You all right?'

He took her hand, and together they ran through the Post, which seemed to be quite full of men with torches, shouting and running, towards the museum. This was also full of policemen. They went past the Siamese twins, past the brains and came to where the case of bladders lay in pieces on the floor; beyond it the door stood open. Framed in the doorway, with the light behind him making an aura of his golden hair, stood the old gentleman with Milly in his arms.

'We've got Winthrop all right,' said Rudolph, 'what about your two?'

Sophia was busy kissing Milly, who showed enthusiasm at the sight of her owner.

'She looks a little bit all eyes,' she said; 'otherwise quite well. Oh, Milly, I do love you.'

'Florence and Heatherley have scuttled themselves in the main drain,' said Sir Ivor, 'and I could do with a whisky and soda, old dears.'

Chapter Fifteen

RUDOLPH had only just been in time. He confessed
that when he first read Sophia's message on the handkerchief he had felt excessively bored. Every woman in
London seemed to have some secret service activity on
hand. Then he remembered that Sophia's manner had
been rather queer, and that, although she must have
known who Mrs. Twitchett was, she had not given him
so much as a wink, even when they were outside the
Post. She was looking white and strained and anxious,
and the circumstance of her having the handkerchief
ready to give him was peculiar. Finally there was something about the way she had worded her message that
made him think this was, after all, no silly joke, but an
affair which called for some investigation.

Accordingly, when he had divested himself of his
Twitchett personality and was once more respectable
in uniform, he hurried round to Scotland Yard with the
handkerchief which he showed, rather deprecatingly, to
Inspector McFarlane. The Inspector, however, so far
from laughing at him, was exceedingly interested. He
told Rudolph that for a long time now the authorities
had suspected that the old 'King' was broadcasting in
this country; that furthermore, Scotland Yard was
on the track of three dangerous spies, the leaders
of a large and well organized gang who were
known to be in London and who so far could not be

located. Quite a lot had been discovered about their activities, but nobody had any idea who they might be or where to find them. Rudolph told him about Florence, of how he had jokingly suggested that she was really a spy, and of the pigeon in her bedroom, and the Inspector, who was quite interested to hear all this, said that the Boston Brotherhood, or any such cranky society, and an American accent would provide an admirable smoke-screen for clever spies. He also said that the gang he was looking for certainly used pigeons, two of which had been shot down over the Channel quite recently.

The long and the short of it was that the Inspector told his two best men that they must somehow penetrate into the cellars of St. Anne's. He advised Rudolph on no account to make any attempt at communicating with Sophia until they knew more, as her life might easily be endangered if he did.

'By the way,' he said, glancing once again at the handkerchief, 'who is Milly?'

'Milly,' said Rudolph angrily, for this made him look a fool, 'since you ask me, is a blasted bitch.'

'A friend of Lady Sophia's?'

'You misunderstand me, Inspector. No, her French bulldog. She is potty about the wretched animal, and certainly if anyone wanted to get Sophia into his power an infallible way would be by kidnapping Milly.'

'I see. So my men must look out (unless the whole thing is a joke) for Sir Ivor King and a French bulldog. If it should prove to be a joke, you must in no way distress yourself, Mr. Jocelyn. In war-time we are bound

to explore every avenue, whether it is likely to be productive of results, or not. Every day we follow up false
clues, and think ourselves lucky if something turns out
to be genuine once in a hundred times. I am very grateful to you for coming round, and will let you know of
course if there are any developments.'

Rudolph went to the Ritz from Scotland Yard, and
here he saw Olga, who was telling quite a little crowd
of people that she was hot-foot on the track of a gang
of dangerous spies, and soon hoped to be able, single-
handed, to deliver them over to justice. Mary Pencill
was also there, assuring her admirers that Russia's
interest in Finland was only that of a big brother, not,
she said, that she held any brief for the present ruler of
Russia, who had shown his true colours the day he
accepted the overtures of Hitler.

In the middle of the night, Inspector McFarlane sent
for Rudolph to go and see him. He had some news. One
of his men had actually seen the King of Song in his subterranean cubby-hole; not only that, he had managed
to hold a short whispered conversation with him. Sir
Ivor told him that the gang had now entirely dispersed
with the exception of Florence, Heatherley and Winthrop. Florence was planning to leave for Germany,
taking Sir Ivor with her, the following day at 8 p.m. An
hour later, a time fuse, which was already in one of the
cellars, would go off, setting in motion an elaborate net-
work of machinery connected with the whole drainage
system of London. Every drain would be blown up,
carrying with it, of course, hundreds of buildings and
streets; the confusion and loss of life would be pro-

digious, the more so as none of the bombs would explode simultaneously, and people hurrying to safety from one part of the town to another would find themselves in the middle of fresh explosions. London would lie a total wreck, and prove an easy prey for the fleet upon fleet of aeroplanes which would now pour over it, dropping armed parachutists. Taking advantage of the city's disorganization, and led by Heatherley and Winthrop, they would soon be in possession of it. London would be destroyed and in enemy hands, the war as good as lost.

'So, you see,' remarked the Inspector, 'it was just as well that you did not treat Lady Sophia's message as a joke. Oh, and by the way, Sir Ivor has the dog with him. He says her snoring gets on his nerves.'

'I'm not surprised. What anybody wants to have a dog like that for——!'

The Inspector told Rudolph that he had better become Mrs. Twitchett again and go to the Post. Like this he would be able to keep an eye on Florence and also to reassure Sophia, whose nerves, if nothing were done to relieve her anxiety, might give way, greatly to the detriment of the Inspector's plans. He wanted to leave the gang undisturbed until nearly the last minute, as it was important that no message should get through to Berlin which would prevent the now eagerly awaited arrival of the parachutists. The War Office was seething with arrangements for their reception.

Everything went off beautifully except that the fusing of the lights, a pure accident, had enabled Florence and Heatherley to dive into the main drain before they could be arrested. It had happened just as the Inspector's men were pouring into the Post through the ordinary entrance and also by means of the drain, and had momentarily caused some confusion.

'We should have preferred to catch them alive,' said the Inspector, 'but there it is.'

Sophia was rather pleased; the idea of Florence as Mata Hari in her silver foxes was repugnant to her, and besides, it would have been embarrassing for Luke. Far better like this.

Presently the air was filled with Dracula-like forms descending slowly through the black-out. These young fellows, the cream of the German army, met with a very queer reception. Squads of air-raid wardens, stretcher-bearers, boy scouts, shop assistants and black-coated workers awaited them with yards and yards of twine, and when they were still a few feet from the earth, tied their dangling legs together. Trussed up like turkeys for the Christmas market, they were bundled into military lorries and hurried away to several large Adam houses which had been commandeered for the purpose. Soon all the newspapers had photographs of them smoking their pipes before a cheery log fire, with a picture of their Führer gazing down at them from the chimney-piece. Sir Ivor King went several times to sing German folk songs with them, a gesture that was much appreciated by the great British public who regarded them with a sort of patronizing affection, rather as if they were members of an Australian cricket team which had come over here and competed, unsuccessfully, for the Ashes.

Chapter Sixteen

SOPHIA was not acclaimed as a national heroine. The worthy burghers of London, who should have been grateful to her, were quite displeased to learn that, although their total destruction had in fact been prevented, this had been done in such an off-hand way, and with so small a margin of time to spare. Sophia was criticized, and very rightly so, for not having called in Scotland Yard the instant she had first seen Florence letting a pigeon out of her bedroom window. Had the full story of her incompetence emerged, had the facts about Milly seen the light of day, it is probable that the windows of 98 Granby Gate would have shared the fate of those at Vocal Lodge, which were now being mended, in gratitude and remorse, at the expense of all the residents of Kew Green. Actually, Sophia was damned with faint praise in the daily press, and slightly clapped when she appeared on the News Reels.

In any case, the King of Song had now soared to such an exalted position in the hearts of his fellow-countrymen that there would hardly have been room for anybody else. Wherever he showed his face in public, even in the Turkish bath, he was snatched up and carried shoulder high; the taxi he had modestly hired to take him from the Ritz, where he had spent the night after being rescued, to Vocal Lodge, was harnessed with laurel ropes to a team of A.T.S., who dragged him there

178

through dense, hysterical crowds. The journey took two and a half hours. He arrived at Vocal Lodge simultaneously with Lady Beech's three van-loads of furniture which she was most thoughtfully re-lending him. Larch, overcome with shame at the recollection of his own Peter-like behaviour, was sobbing on the doorstep; the glaziers were still at work on the windows, and in fact, the whole place was so disorganized that Sir Ivor got back into the taxi, very much hoping that it would be allowed to return under its own steam. The taxi man, however, glad of the opportunity to save petrol, signalled to the local decontamination squad who seized the ropes and dragged it back to the Ritz. This journey, owing to the fact that the decontamination squad was in full gas-proof clothing and service masks, took three and a half hours, and one of them died of heart failure in the bar soon after the arrival.

All the secrets of the German espionage system were now as an open book to the astute old singer, who had had the opportunity of looking through many secret documents during the course of his captivity and had committed everything of importance to memory. Not for nothing had he the reputation of being able to learn a whole opera between tea and dinner. Codes, maps of air bases, army plans, naval dispositions, all were now in the hands of the M.I.; while the arrangements for the occupation of England, perfect to every detail, were issued in a White Paper, much to the delight of the general public.

It was universally admitted that Sir Ivor had played his cards brilliantly. When Winthrop, alias Gustav, had approached him, shortly before the outbreak of war, with the offer of a huge sum if he would lend his services to Germany, he had seen at once that here was a wonderful opportunity to help his country. He had accepted, partly, as he told Winthrop, because he needed the money, and partly because he was a firm believer in slavery. Then, very cleverly, he had resisted the temptation to communicate with Scotland Yard before disappearing; had he done so, the Eiweisses, through certain highly-placed officials now languishing in the Tower, would inevitably have found out, and the 'murder' of the old gentleman would have been one indeed.

The Eiweisses, close friends of Hitler, had been preparing their position since the Munich *putsch* of 1923, and as Heatherley Egg and Florence Turnbull were quite well-known citizens of the United States, and the most trusted lieutenants of Brother Bones. They were known to be bores, on both sides of the Atlantic; more sinister attributes had never been suspected, least of all by the worthy Brother himself. In the end they seemed to have been undone by a sort of childish naïveté. Sir Ivor could always dispel, as soon as they arose, any doubts of his *bona fides* by talking to them of his old music teacher at Düsseldorf, of the German Christmas which he loved so much, of the duel he had fought as a student, and his memories of the old beer cellar. He aroused a nostalgia in their souls for the fatherland, and thus he lulled any suspicions which they might otherwise have had. Picture the delight with which his fellow-citizens now learnt of his duplicity. The old music teacher (long since dead, the broadcast, like the duet with Frau Goering, had been a hoax) was really a Polish Jew, the 'King' detested beer, he had never spent a Christmas in Germany, and the scar on his temple, which, so he had told the von Eiweisses, was the result of a duel, had really been acquired in a bicycling accident many years ago when he had toured the Isle of Wight with the posthumous Duchess and Lady Beech, in bloomers.

As for Rudolph, while everybody admitted the value of his work, nobody could forbear to smile; the public took him to their hearts as a sort of Charley's Aunt, and he soon figured in many a music-hall joke. His colonel sent for him and drew his attention to the rule that officers should not appear in mufti during war-time.

Sophia gave a dinner party in honour of the King of Song and of Luke's safe return from America. It was a large party. The guests included Lady Beech, Fred and Ned and their wives, Mary Pencill, Sister Wordsworth, the Gogothskas, Rudolph, a girl called Ruth whom Luke had met on the clipper and who was now staying in Florence's room at 98 Granby Gate, and, of course, the King of Song himself in the very wig which had been found by the innocent gambollers of Kew Green, and which he had borrowed for the evening from the Scotland Yard museum of horrors.

Olga arrived late enough to be certain of being last, but not so late that dinner would have been started without her. Years of practice enabled her to hit off the right moment. She was in the uniform of her important war work, and wore a small tiara which she had bought back from the American who had bought it from Serge's father. It bore historic associations, having belonged, so she alleged, to Catharine the Great, one of whose lovers one of Serge's ancestors, of course, had been. Sophia had once caused very bad feeling by asking whether the diamonds were yellow with age or whether Catharine the Great had been disappointed in Serge's ancestor. Olga now made herself the centre of attention by the announcement that she was leaving almost at once for Kurdistan, on a very important mission.

'To-morrow,' she said, 'I go down to Suffolk to say adieu to Moushka; early next week I leave.'

Moushka was old Mrs. Bagg. In Olga's pre-Russian days she had been known as Mummie, which had been all right for the mother of Baby Bagg. Princess Olga Gogothsky required a Moushka. Serge, on the other hand, always called his parents Pa and Ma; but then he pronounced his own name, as did all his friends, like that stuff of which schoolgirls' skirts are made. Olga gave it a very different sound—'Sairgay'.

'I suppose, now that Sophia has caught all the spies in London, there is nothing much left for you to do here,' said Rudolph, loyally.

'Spies!' The Princess gave a scornful twist to her lips as though spies were enormously beneath her attention, nowadays. 'No, I have important business to do there, for my Chief, with the Kahns.'

Nobody asked who the Kahns were.

Serge was in the seventh heaven. It seemed that, by dint of enlisting under an assumed name and as a private, he had managed to get back to his Blossom.

Determined not to lose his love a second time, he was now on the water-waggon, but even this experiment had not damped his spirits, and he appeared to be the happiest living Russian.

Fred and Ned had once more reversed positions. Ned had proved to be even more of a failure at the Ministry than Britain had expected he would, and there had been, the day before Sophia's dinner, a Cabinet purge during which Ned was sent off to try his luck in another place. As we do not yet live under a totalitarian régime, this other place was, of course, that English equivalent of the grave, the House of Lords. Meanwhile, Fred, reinstated in both popular and Ministerial esteem by the triumphant return of Sir Ivor King, was back at his old job. This exchange was, luckily, to the satisfaction of both parties. Ned's wife had for some time been making his nights hideous with her complaints and assertions that at her age (she was nearly thirty) it was quite un-heard of not to be a peeress and made her look ridicu-lous, while Fred had never taken to Blossom with Serge's ardour and had really been hankering after that Cabinet key all the time.

Fred and Sir Ivor were soon discussing the campaign of Song Propaganda which was to be launched the following week.

'We must especially concentrate, of course, on bigger and better Pets' Programmes than ever before,' said the Minister.

'You're joking!'

'What? Indeed I am not.'

'Of course the Pets' Programmes were simply put in

to tease the Germans,' said Sir Ivor, 'and I also hoped they would show people here that the whole thing was bogus.'

'Then you very much under-estimated our English love for dumb animals,' Fred replied pompously. 'Let me tell you that the Pets' Programmes were the only ones the Government were really worried about—why, every man, woman and dog in the whole country listened to those wretched programmes. You should have seen, for instance, how much Abbie and Milly enjoyed them. They never missed one. Why, entirely owing to you, there is now a Pets' League of Peace and Slavery, with literally thousands of members. The Pets wear awful little badges and pay half-a-crown. They had a mammoth meeting last week in the Dell at Hyde Park.'

'We'll soon alter that,' said the old gentleman. 'I will start a Society for Patriotic Pets and make them pay five bob.'

'Please will you two come in to dinner.'

Sophia sat between the King of Song and Luke, because, as she explained, she had not yet had a word with Luke since his return. 'We shall have to have the Clipper,' she said in an undertone to her godfather, who quite understood. They had it. After a bit they were able to leave Luke and Ruth having it together, with Lady Beech, who, like the Athenians, loved new things, lending an occasional ear. The pink sunrise, the pink sunset, the next pink sunrise and the food.

Sophia asked Sir Ivor about Agony 22, but he was quite as much in the dark about the great egg mystery as Heatherley had been.

'Come now, pretty young lady,' he said. 'How could I get at your egg?'

'I know, but in spy stories people seem to manage these things.'

Ned here chimed in with the news that many eggs nowadays have things written on them.

'I expect there is a farm called Agony, and that egg was laid in 1922,' he said.

'But why should there be a farm called Agony?'

'You never can tell; farms are called some very queer things. When I was Under-Secretary for Agriculture——'

'By the way, Sophie, you must be feeling a bit easier on the subject of parachutists, eh?' asked Fred. Anything to stop Ned from telling about when he was Under-Secretary for Agriculture.

'Well, yes, but there's such an awful new horror; I think of nothing else. I read in some paper that the Germans are employing midget spies, so small that they can hide in a drawer, and the result is I simply daren't look for a hanky nowadays.'

'Don't worry; we've caught nearly all of them. The Government are issuing an appeal to-morrow for old dolls' houses to keep them in.'

Lady Beech, having heard the Clipper out to the last throb of its engines, now collected a few eyes, for she liked general conversation, leant across the table, and said to her brother-in-law, 'Tell me, Ivor, dear, what sort of a life did you have under the First Aid Post?'

'Oh yes,' said all the others, 'do tell us how it was.'

'Spiffing,' said the old Edwardian. 'They fitted up a

Turkish bath for me, and I spent hours of every day in that. Then one member of the gang (I expect you would remember him, Sophie, a stretcher-bearer called Wolf) used to be a hairdresser on one of those liners, and he brushed my—er—scalp in quite a special way, to induce baby growth. And by jingo he induced it!' And sure enough Sir Ivor snatched off his wig and proudly exhibited some horrible little bits of white fluff. 'After all these years,' he said. 'I was stone bald at thirty, you know; the man must be a genius. He is now in the Tower and I am making an application at the Home Office to be allowed to visit him once a week, for treatment. It is all I ask in return for my, not inconsiderable, services.'

'Tell me, Ivor, did you not feel most fearfully anxious when the weeks passed and you had no communication with the outside world?'

'Rather not. I know how stupid Germans are, you see—felt certain they would give themselves away sooner or later, and sure enough they did and everything was O.K. just as I always guessed it would be.'

'Bit touch and go?' said Luke.

'Keep your hair on,' said the old Singer. 'A miss is as good as a mile, ain't it?'